Praise for *Crazy*

"Joey El Bueno recalls his childhood in World War II–era New York in this nostalgic, uncharacteristically sentimental novel from horror movie master Blatty."

—*The Sunday Denver Post*

"Sassy humor and gentle nostalgia is the surprisingly effective combination employed by Blatty in this fond look back at 1940s-era New York. [Readers] will be treated to an entertaining romp through the Lower East Side conducted by an inimitable tour guide."

—*Booklist*

"There's a certain vaudevillian flair to all of Blatty's work, but it's the sort of vaudeville that powers the absurdist despair of Samuel Beckett's *Waiting for Godot;* one-liners and gags are just another way to deal with the inevitability of death. The difference is, there's a core of faith and optimism at the heart of Blatty's writing. Horror exists, as do evil and the monsters who perpetuate it, but there's also God in his heaven, purpose, and at least the possibility of justice."

—*The Onion*

Crazy

WILLIAM PETER BLATTY

A TOM DOHERTY ASSOCIATES BOOK
NEW YORK

CRAZY

A Tor Book
Published by Tom Doherty Associates, LLC
175 Fifth Avenue
New York, NY 10010

www.tor-forge.com

Tor® is a registered trademark of Tom Doherty Associates, LLC.

ISBN 978-0-7653-6664-1

First Edition: November 2010
First Mass Market Edition: October 2011

Printed in the United States of America

0 9 8 7 6 5 4 3 2 1

For Julie and Paul

Only if we know that the thing which truly matters is the infinite can we avoid fixing our interest upon futilities, and upon all kinds of goals which are not of real importance.

—Carl Jung
Memories, Dreams, Reflections

Hell is the inability to love.

—Fyodor Dostoevsky
The Brothers Karamazov

Crazy

1

Where do I begin? The seventh grade at St. Stephen's on East 28th Street in 1941, I suppose, because that's where and when I first met Jane, back before we grew up and she started disappearing and then reappearing in someplace like Tibet or Trucial Oman from where she'd send me picture postcards with tiny scrawled messages in different-colored inks such as, "Thinking of you sometimes in the morning" or "Angkor Wat really smells. Joey, don't ever come here for a vacation," but there'd be only a day between the postmarked dates and sometimes no difference at all between them, and then all of a sudden she'd reappear again looking years younger, which is nothing, I suppose, when compared to that time when supposedly she levitated six feet off the ground when she thought they were running out of Peter Paul Mounds candy bars at the refreshment counter of the old Superior movie house on 30th Street and Third Avenue back when there were el trains rumbling overhead and a nickel got you two or three feature films, plus a Buck Jones Western chapter, four cartoons, bingo and an onstage paddleball contest, when supposedly a theater usher approached her and told her, "Hey, come on, kid, get down, you can't be doing that crazy stuff in here!" and right away she wobbled down to the seedy lobby carpet, gave the usher the arm and yelled, "That's the same kind of crap they gave Tinkerbell!" but then I know you have no interest in any of these matters, so fine, let's by all means move on and go back to the beginning.

Which comes at the end.

"Medication time."

It's December 24, 2010, and I'm sitting by a window in a tenth-floor Bellevue Hospital recovery room staring down at a tugboat churning up a foaming white *V* at its prow in the East River's death-dark suicide waters and looking like it's hugging itself against the cold. "Hi ya, kiddo!" The tubby and diminutive Nurse Bloor breezily waddles into my room, a hypodermic syringe upraised in her pudgy little staph-infested fingers. She stops by my chair and I look down at her feet and I stare. I've never seen a nurse in stiletto heels. She glances over at something I sculpted a couple of days before and says, "Hey, now, what's that?" and I tell her that it's Father Perrault's wooden leg from *Lost Horizon*, but she doesn't pursue it, nor does she react to my laptop computer: she has read *Archy and Mehitabel* and knows that sometimes even a rat can type.

"Okay, a teensy little stick," she says.

I yelp, "Ouch!"

"Oh, come on, now, don't tell me that hurt!"

Well, it didn't, but I want to puncture her starched-white pride and maddening air of self-assurance. She scowls, slaps a Band-Aid on the puncture and leaves. Sometimes growth of the soul needs pain, which is something I have always been on the spot to give.

The pneumatic door closes with a sigh. I turn my glance to my desk and the gift from Bloor that's sitting on top of it, a foot-tall artificial Christmas tree with different-colored Band-Aids hanging from its branches. For a moment I stare at it dully, and then I shift my gaze to the dry and abandoned public pool down on the corner of First Avenue and 23rd where I almost drowned when Paulie Farragher and Jimmy Connelly kept shoving me back into the pool's deep end every time I tried to climb up and out for air and I swore any number of choking, coughing blood oaths that if God let me live I would track them to Brazil or to China or the Yucatán, anyplace at all where I could offer them death without the comfort of the sacraments. Yes. I remember all of that. I do. I remember even though I'm eighty-two years old.

Again.

2

"Are you Joey El Bueno?"

I was packing up my book bag after class when I looked up and saw this really pretty girl with reddish hair that she wore in pigtails with green-and-yellow smiley-face barrettes at the ends.

"Yeah, that's me," I said. "Why?"

"So *you're* the one!" she exclaimed.

The girl's jade green eyes were slowly tracing all over my face with a look of awe, if not loony adoration.

I said, "I'm the one what?"

She said, "The Mask!"

Instantly I knew that this girl was crazy.

"The Mask" referred to something I had done in fifth grade. We had this new teacher, Miss Comiskey, a pretty nineteen-year-old who had never before taught a course in anything unless it was absolute futility, and who seemed thoroughly convinced that our only path to knowledge was in reciting some fact at least one hundred times, such as "Lake Titicaca is the largest lake in South America." Bad enough, but even worse when our tall, wrinkled, thin-lipped principal, old gaunt-faced Sister Veronica, walked in like some animated withered leaf for a check on how Comiskey was getting along and the boys in the class couldn't make it through the word "Titicaca" without totally losing it, which of course was pretty much a big nothing when compared to the quiet, ever-overhanging terror all the boys in the class had to live with the following year when our teacher was a nun and she'd ask us questions and we'd have to stand up to give the answer at a time in our lives when almost anything—the swish of a dress, hearing someone in the street saying

"Tondelayo," which was the name of Hedy Lamarr's character in *White Cargo*—might produce an instantaneous and irrepressible outward sign of our interest, such as happened quite often with the hot-blooded Johnny Baloqui, the tall and dramatic-looking Spaniard among us, and I can still see him standing there, his eyes wide with panic, and yet always with his chin held proudly high in some awesomely courageous but doomed attempt at projecting matador haughtiness and cool while he stood there like a stork with his right leg lifted high and bent inward toward his crotch in this ludicrous Marx Brothers effort at concealment, while at the same time assuring the nun in charge in quiet tones that "General Wolfe defeated General Montcalm in the Battle of Quebec in 1759." Once he'd looked off pensively and frowned as he added in a murmur, "At least I *think* that's the date."

This last was Baloqui's attempt at *Gaslight*.

So now, "The Mask," I echoed dully.

"The Mask."

Driven stark raving mad by the endless

recitations in Comiskey's class, I played "the hook" for a week, smashing open a piggy bank with a leftover, rock-hard, four-day-old frozen tamale that Pop had concocted for Sunday dinner and then going to Times Square to see first-run movies like *Gulliver's Travels*, which wouldn't get to the Superior for six more years, but not having the instincts of Jean Valjean I got caught red-handed when my father, in a break from habit, decided to pick me up from school for no rational reason that I could divine, unless it was to vault me to the head of the list of "Top Ten Stupidest Grammar School Criminals." So it was back to Miss Comiskey and her "Give Me the Boy and I'll Give You Back His Remains" school of learning, which was doubtless the inspiration for future North Korean interrogation techniques. Well, I took it for another two weeks until one rainy Monday morning when I took my seat in the back of the room, folded my hands on top of my desk and sat silent and motionless and looking straight ahead while ignoring the excited whoops and giggles and chatter all around me. I was wearing a frighteningly realistic wraparound mask of Joseph Merrick, the "Elephant Man." In fourth grade Sister Joseph had made us study his picture to show us how freaking well-off we all were and to quit complaining about the piled-on home-work, and so after much practice making masks of Dick Tracy, Barney Google and Maggie and Jiggs out of cutouts provided by the *Sunday Journal-American*, my hands had fairly leapt to the Merrick Challenge and I waited now, silent and unmoving, for Comiskey to come into the room, which she soon enough did, and I've got to say the first reviews were a rave: first the "Eeek!" and the electrified raised hair just like Little Orphan Annie in the comics, then the shouts and the orders and hysterical threats of what would happen unless I took off the mask *"right now!"* But I didn't. I just sat there like a statue, still looking straight ahead with my hands clasped and resting on the top of my desk. Sister Louise would by now have been whacking my knuckles with a ruler until I'd clearly grasped the limits of innovation, but my silence and statue-like, eerie lack of motion—not to mention the mask—unnerved

Comiskey to the point that her hands were shaking. She bolted from the room and came back with Sister Veronica, who after taking one look at me dismissed the class and sent down for Miss Doyle, her office assistant, because Doyle had studied psychology in school. Just a little under four feet tall, Doyle had worn the same ratty pink cardigan sweater every day for all the years that I'd been at St. Stephen's, plus this foot-long, huge wooden cross that dangled from a metal chain of thorns around her neck. There was also the matter of her dyed-green hair. She gimped into the room, took me in with a glance, and then, folding her arms across her chest, turned to Sister Veronica and said, "Why am I here?"

I took off the mask. It was an act of reverence.

Smiling thinly, the nun turned to Comiskey. "You see?"

The second time this happened in the future-past, right after I'd taken off the mask I blew the three women's minds by intoning, "He who offers no resistance is irresistible," a quote from Siddhartha Gautama I'd seen framed on a local public library wall. At the words, Sister Veronica clutched at her beads, no doubt thinking of calling in a priest, while Miss Doyle took a prudent half step backward. Miss Comiskey said, "What in shit is this?" one hundred times.

• • •

"What made you do it?" this girl Jane was asking me now.

Because I didn't want to go through all the stuff about Comiskey, I looked away, gave a shrug and said, "I learn from the sky."

"Oh, my God, you *are* 'the one'!" I heard her breathing out ecstatically as if she'd just found her long-lost lucky rock. I turned and saw that goofy look of adoration again and I could see that she hadn't meant "the one." She meant "The *One!*"

"The one *what?*" I asked just to be sure.

"The one who's going to help me find the Secret Christmas Gift."

"Find the *what?*"

"Never mind. It's not important right now. What's important is some advice I need to give you. It might even save your life."

I said, "Listen, who are you, okay? You want to tell me?"

"Call me Jane," she said. "Jane Bent. I'm an eighth-grade transfer from Our Lady of Sorrows. You don't remember me with Farragher that day? I saw you watching."

I put my fingers to my chin.

"Oh, yeah, right. So that was you?"

I'd seen her in the school yard approaching Paulie Farragher and shaking his hand. Wearing his trademark dark blue winter overcoat that was so oversized you couldn't ever see his hands, he'd just been in a fight with a big eighth-grader in which he had mounted his usual revolutionary defensive technique of wildly flailing his arms back and forth in a furious windmilling motion so that any opponent couldn't possibly penetrate it, and most times didn't even want to, stepping back to stare at Farragher with disawe, which is a mixture of awe and disbelief, and deciding he was probably mentally unbalanced. When I'd asked what Jane had said to him, he'd shrugged and said, "Nothing. Nothing really. She just shook my hand and said, 'Nice.'"

"And so what is it?" I was asking Jane now. "What's this advice?"

"You know those super-deadly bombs going off in your class?" she said in this portentous but quiet, even tone.

"Yeah, I do. How do *you* know about them?"

"I just know. They're coming from Rosemary Pagliarello. She sits near you in the back of the room. Change your seat. Sit up front. Her bombs are deadly and I need you for the Christmas Quest!" At that I had to quickly look around for this nutty girl's keepers: you know, great big guys in white coats with huge butterfly nets at the ready, always smiling and happy to be chloroforming some kid. Then my eyes settled back on Bent. Something told me right then that I ought to walk away. But I didn't. There was something so magnetic about her. Something deep.

"And since when can inner sanctum weapons kill?" I asked her, trying hard to look studiously interested and not like I was talking to a borderline psycho, which was actually what I was thinking.

"Since Rosemary got taken over."

"What do you mean?"

"She's one of *them* now."

"One of who?"

"The Others."

I didn't dare take a big step backward, which, I swear, is what I desperately wanted to do, but I was scared it might trigger some kind of attack, like by some wounded and dope-crazed Chihuahua, so I just stood there sort of stroking my chin in an effort to look thoughtful and evenhanded. I said, "Yes, Jane, I see it now. 'Them.' Rosemary's bombs. It's all adding up. I mean, there's something really spooky about her output, a 'not of this world' kind of thing," I observed. "And yet I haven't seen anyone in class fall over dead. That's the strange thing about it. Don't you think?"

Exasperated, Jane shook her head and then leaned in, her face about an inch from mine as she throatily whispered, "Joey, haven't you been listening? You're *The One!* Rosemary's bombs are all 'smart bombs.' They're programmed to target only *you!* Yeah, well sure, they can miss by a yard or two, maybe, and then some nun's going to get it. Too bad. Now will you quit it with these rationalizations? I mean, come on, Joey! Don't be so naïve!"

She was getting worked up a bit, her green eyes wider and her cheeks turning pink, and this whole conversation, if that's what you call it, was of course reinforcing my original suspicion that she might be two incense censers short of a Benediction. "Okay, then, prove that I'm wrong," she demanded, "and, oh please, wipe that smirk off your face, would you, Joey? That was always so creepy and unattractive."

"What did you say?"

"It's so creepy and unattractive!"

No. She said *"was."*

I let it go and said, "I can't."

"You can't what? Prove I'm wrong or get rid of the smirk?"

I said, "Both." And then suddenly her face brightened up with a smile like the rising of the moon as she appraised me proudly and warmly and said, "Nice. It was a test of trust and you passed. All that stuff about

Rosemary's bombs was baloney. I made it up. But you believed me, Joey. You *trusted*. Want to go for a Coke?"

I felt three things all at once, the first being shame that in fact I hadn't *really* ever fully trusted anyone, while another was a curious disappointment that this girl wasn't actually nuttier than a truckload of filberts, as I guess I was perverse enough to find a little lunacy incredibly attractive. But the third thing, the bad thing that I felt, was flummoxed panic. Everybody knew back then that the boy paid, while "going Dutch" meant wearing stupid wooden shoes; but I had no cash, not even the quarter a day that Pop gave me for my lunches, enough to buy me five small fresh-baked rolls and a bowl of Manhattan clam chowder at Fiorenza's Bakery at the corner of Third and 28th. Because my father pushed a hot dog cart in the winter and an ice cream cart in the summer, you could say that we were more or less comfortably destitute, so that while fun was available in lots of differ-ent ways, not one of them required filthy lucre, the most carefree and breeziest time of my life up to then being fourth grade when it was always good for a rush to tap on the all-glass front of the Chinese laundry on the corner of Lexington and 29th, and then hold up a hand with all your fingers splayed out while with the other you made this quick, slicing motion across your throat, which the almond-eyed guys with the puzzled stare and the pigtails and the red-hot flatirons gripped in their hands were supposed to understand was code for "Chinese eat rats on Friday!" which Farragher, for one, didn't learn wasn't factually correct until graduate school at CCNY, which is neither here nor there, I suppose, so getting back now to the subject of cost-free fun, hitching rides on the backs of American Express trucks was also a ragingly popular choice. Still another was to have one of my pals come up behind me as I walked downhill on 34th Street toward Lexington Avenue and first pretend to steal my wallet, then viciously club me over the head with a piece of lead pipe, whereupon I would crumple to the sidewalk like a boiled noodle while my buddy ran away. Then, *"No! No police!"*

I would hysterically yell when I supposedly came to, my eyes wide and bulging out in terror as if I were an escapee from a criminal youth farm, and I'd quickly leap up and tear away uphill to Park Avenue, disappearing around the corner with an ululating, heart-rending shriek of *"No police!"* which gave an even bigger rush than finding the words "Lucky Stick" on the slim wooden handle of your five-cent Popsicle, which got you another one for free. There were also the summers when my best friend, Tommy Foley, and I would play handball in the blazing sun for endless hours at the public park on East 37th, right after which, exhausted and dripping sweat, we would stumble on up to the Kips Bay Boys Club where we'd strip down naked—those were the rules—and from the deep-end diving board we'd let ourselves limply fall into the pool, and when our over-heated bodies slipped into those velvety icy-cool waters we would feel an intense and all-enveloping bodily pleasure as well as something deeper and indescribable but which felt very much like justice, and for these few fleeting moments of immersive contact with the Great and All-powerful Oz, we would more than gladly torture ourselves on the handball court for hours most days of the summer. It was all for that first deep dive.

It never seemed to work for the second.

3

Poor Pop. He tried. Two summers before, in 1939, he took me out on a Sunday to the New York World's Fair, where all the exhibits were free. I was really excited to go inasmuch as I'd just finished reading "World's Fair Goblin" in *Doc Savage Magazine*, which like all of my magazine and comic book reading was done standing up in the magazine section at Boshnack's Cigarette and Candy shop near the corner of Third and 35th. Pop gave me a quarter and then let me moose around the fairgrounds for a while on my own—I think he'd spotted a pavilion with some other old guys there playing chess and maybe even a PERUVIANS WELCOME sign. The first thing I went to for an up-close look was the Fair's famous symbols, these enormous white modernistic structures—one a thin, tall obelisk called the Trylon and the other, right beside it, a huge white ball called the Perisphere. Cool. But some of the free things in life aren't the best, and no exhibit that I went to was great, in particular Bell Telephone's. It being mid-morning, I guess, there was nobody else around and I took this hearing test where you put on headphones and listened to these tiny electronic beeps that dwindled down to a point where only high-school hall monitors in Prussia and a certain breed of mongoose could possibly hear them, and when I handed in my test paper showing that I thought I'd heard every single beep, the young gum-chewing girl who graded it looked up at me with total disbelief, if not revulsion. "You heard every single *one?*" she sneered, and when I told her, "Yes, I did," this demonic, taunting look shone out of her eyes and as if in an effort to smoke me out she said in this barely audible whisper, "You're a fucking little liar!" I stood there powerfully wishing for the gift of speaking horrifically "in tongues," or of being Superman with no scruples as I had an idea of where the Trylon might go, but all I did was say, "Actually, I'm big for my age. Could I please have my test paper back?" And then there was "Bring 'Em Back Alive" Frank Buck, the world-famous wild animal trapper. Just outside the entrance to his huge tented "Jungle-Land Camp," there he was sitting on a stool in his "For God and Empire" bush shirt and shorts, not to mention his trademark "Doctor Livingston, You Putz, I Presume" pith helmet. No one else was around, only me and Buck and this dopey-eyed, pathetic-looking teenaged elephant standing there a few feet away from him, no doubt waiting for its daily dose of gingko biloba as it watched him eating something out of a bowl which we were all supposed to think was Kikuyu stew, I guess, but which the eye of an El Bueno could detect was a thick tortilla soup. Just then a fine drizzle of rain began to fall. It was so quiet I could hear Buck's spoon scraping around in the bowl. He stopped chewing, maybe sensing my adenoidal, breathy presence, and he turned his head and met my stare with a look that seemed half appreciation for my presence and half apology to this kid for diminishing his dashing, adventurous image with this crummy exhibit so he could keep making mortgage payments on his tree house. Looking sad-eyed, he turned back to his lunch.

The other exhibits were just as boring. Pop once told me, "Do not say to me ever, 'I am bored,' because if you are bored is most probably because you are boring person." Fine, then. Guilty as charged. The boring exhibits, meantime, as Arrigo once famously said about his failure to graduate on time, were "a mere bag of shells" among the day's tribulations, all because I would swoon when I passed by one of these hamburger stands that, I swear, would pop up about every fifty feet with their maddening aromas of mustard, greasy beef, and sweet relish, but at fifty cents apiece they were out of the question and my choices were to faint in front of one of the stands—preferably at the feet of some woman wearing diamonds and could double as Ingrid Bergman playing a nun in *The Bells of St. Mary's*—or to contemplate certain more desperate measures winding up in the headlines of the evening papers:

WORLD'S FAIR HAMBURGER VENDOR MAIMED IN ASSAULT. BERSERK YOUNG ATTACKER AT LARGE

Then in smaller print underneath:

**Buns, Grilled Meat Taken. Hot
Spatula Thought to Be Weapon**

Never mind. Like I said: Pop tried.

4

"Frozen Milky Ways?" Jane said seductively.

"Oh, well, I'd like to but I can't."

"Why not?"

"Because I haven't got the money," some demon of honesty blurted before I could stop him. Jane shrugged. "Well, okay." She sighed with disappointment and this serious and troubled sort of look on her face. "Then let's go to Fiorenza's and smell hot buns, or would you rather watch lube jobs at Morrie's Auto Works?" And then seeing my reaction, she cascaded into boom-boxed pixie dust laughter. "Hey, come on, I'm just kidding," she said to me, smiling, then she reached into a pocket, flashed a five-dollar bill and said, "See this? I'm loaded."

Five bucks? Was she ever!

It was Friday and a Catholic feast day and classes were out at noon, and so we went to see a movie on East 14th near Third, where every five or six minutes you'd feel the shake of the el trains rumbling overhead. I wasn't sure they would let us in. On the Feast of the Ascension, Foley and I had to sit on an apartment building staircase for almost three hours to see Hedy Lamarr in *White Cargo* on account of the pissy, hard-of-hearing old woman in the ticket booth who thought we were playing the hook. She'd cupped a hand to her ear, her wrinkled face scrunched up and suspicious as she asked, "The feast of *what?*"

"The Ascension," I told her.

"That's a lie. There isn't any Catholic Feast of Consumption." It didn't help that Foley then threatened her with bayonet practice.

Today, though, we didn't get a challenge.

The movie that we wanted to see was *Gunga Din*, but first we had to sit through Movietone News and after that a crummy comedy about Brooklyn, the word "Brooklyn" being the source of all the humor, I gathered, which was zilch, but it was loud with lots of yelling, which was good because we hadn't eaten lunch and my stomach had started to rumble and it being that so far as I knew I was the only human being in the world with this problem, and being wide-eyed with panic that Jane would hear it, I made a sudden quick trip, or so I told her, to the men's room, but just stood in the back of the theater for a while as I waited for my stomach to figure out that it actually wasn't Krakatoa, until an usher came up to me, leaned over and whispered, "Hey, kid, what's the problem?" and thinking he was talking about the rumbling, I blurted, "I was *born* this way! I can't *help* it!" Right. All a part of life's rich pageant. But it all worked out pretty much okay since by the time *Gunga Din* had begun, the stupid rumbling had finally grossed itself out, I guess, because it stopped and I was back in my seat. When *Gunga Din* ended I wanted to see it again, and so did Jane, believe it or not, which I say because the picture was a manly man beer-and-belch, bonding-and-adventure kind of thing, but Jane loved it as much as me and we sat through three showings of that jerky Brooklyn movie just so we could watch *Gunga Din* three times, which, believe me, said a lot of great things about Jane, as much later in life when I took a first-time date to see the movie at some art house that was having a "Cary Grant Week," at the end when Din's on top of the Temple of Gold in a turban and this diaper he's always wearing, and he's blowing a bugle to warn off all these British troops who were approaching wearing kilts and playing bagpipes and singing "Bonnie Laurie," that they're marching directly into an ambush by hordes of fanatical Thugee assassins who are about to shove the bagpipes straight up their butts before feasting and toasting the Goddess Kali with a drink made of cobra blood and Gordon's Dry Gin, this being the closest they could get to a Harvey Wallbanger; but then Din gets shot about a jillion times and as he falls from the top of the temple he keeps trying to blow the warning on the bugle which, sure, since he's dying doesn't sound like

Harry James, and my date put her hand to her mouth and *giggled!*

At that part of the picture Jane cried all three times.

The movie made me thirsty, plus I was starving, so Jane and I decided to get something to eat, but that was only after Jane had to wave off all my phony protestations that I couldn't let her "pay for that too" while all the time I was walking two quick steps ahead as I lured her toward a little Italian restaurant I'd noticed on our way to the film. It turned out that the place was so down on its heels they didn't even have plastic grapes all around, they had *photos* of plastic grapes. We sat down in a booth with a mirrored wall and when I saw that our tablecloth was made of white paper and there were crayons for little kids to doodle around with while they drooled and whined infantile threats for their food, I almost felt sick to my stomach because even to this day I get nauseous at the sight of paint palettes and brushes, even crayons, on account of my older sister, Lourdes, who was terrifically beautiful and later on married and moved to California, but when I was five and she was sixteen she had this endless stream of middle-aged merchants Pop dealt with always coming around to our West Side apartment in some hopeless sort of Old World courting ritual, and always on their first—and always last—sort of audience that Pop had arranged for them, they'd come to the apartment and just sit and have a visit with Pop and me and Lourdes, who'd be sitting the whole time with this look on her face like any second she was going to bolt up from her chair and say, "Excuse me, I have to go shoot myself." The guys were mostly Greek or Lebanese or Armenian, and always wanting to ingratiate themselves with "the kid," every one of them would bring me a gift of the same freaking children's paint set, and soon there were stacks of them piled up in our entry hall closet, which was mostly pretty tough on Lourdes, on account of our bathroom being right off the living room so everyone would hear what she was doing in there, this entry hall closet being farther away, that's where Lourdes would always hurry to after excusing herself for "just a minute," lock herself inside it and throw up.

Once this short, skinny, middle-aged Armenian tailor thought he might break the ice with a tailor joke: "Once dis tailor he put up sign outside his store which is saying, 'A.B. TINK WHATYOUTINK! WE SELL CLOTHES FOR NUTTINK!' Comes den a customer, he is picking out suit and den after he is saying, 'What dis ting you are giving me? A bill?' 'Sure, a bill,' says the tailor in the joke: 'You cannot read what is saying the sign? Is saying, "A.B. TINK. WHAT YOU TINK? WE SELL CLOTHES FOR *NUTTINK?*!' "'"

Lourdes was in the closet for a record eight minutes.

"Oh, hey look," Jane exclaimed with high perk. "All these crayons! Come on, let's both draw something, Joey! What fun!" An entry hall closet door flashed to mind as a possible subject of my sketch, but a waiter came by just then and we ordered spaghetti with meatballs and Jane asked him to bring us "any really, *really* red red wine." They must have thought we were midgets, inasmuch as no problem about age came up, and the waiter brought us glasses of a dark red wine that he *said* was "Tokay." You never know. It tasted velvety, thick and sweet, and as I'd never drunk alcohol before in my life within minutes I was speaking several unknown languages poorly. "I feel like the top of my head's floating off," I told Jane with this idiotic grin on my face that I'm pretty sure lasted the whole time we were there. The wine hit Jane too, I think, because as soon as she was done with her spaghetti she pushed aside her plate, leaned back, and with her hands clasped in front of her on the table and that same spacey look in her eyes that so often graces those of the incontrovertibly boxed, she drawled slurrily, "In the summer I used to raise bees."

I answered woozily, "Neat-o. Where was that? On some farm?"

"Time and space, what do they matter?" she answered; and then staring intently into my eyes she leaned forward with her head close to mine and confided, "It's the bees that count, Joey. It's the bees." As I had no snappy comeback to this, I kept quiet with my stare glazed and dopey and my eyebrows knitting inward in this ludicrous attempt at looking wise and judicious while massively crocked at the age of thirteen and not minding the snickering of angels far away. "I was running out of room for my bees," Jane continued gravely, "so I went to a cigar store and asked the owner if he maybe had an empty cigar box I could have. He said, 'Sure. What do you want it for, kid?' I said, 'Bees. I raise bees. I've got about a thousand that I'm taking to another location; you know, someplace where bees have real meaning for people and they don't go burning crosses smeared with honey on your lawn and screaming, "Keep your creepy hives the hell out of our lives!" and then waving all their medical bills for bee stings. I need the cigar box to put them in,' I told him, and when he said, 'Won't they suffocate, kid?' I said, 'Fuck 'em!' " And with this Jane polished off the last of her wine, banged the glass back down on the table and drilled me with her eyes without a smile or a blink.

"Do you believe that?" she asked me.

Oh, well, first off, even shnockered I had to blink a bit at Jane's salty lingo, though in just a few seconds that feeling went away and the word seemed just a colorful but innocent part of her, like the freckles on the end of her nose. But as for believing her story, no way, although based on Jane's quirkiness, who knew?—plus now the Tokay was putting in its two cents with "Better watch it there, kid! Call her a liar and you'll wind up washing dishes in this dump all day on account of she won't be picking up your tab!" Solid thinking for a not-so-popular wine. But instead of saying, "*Sure,* I believe it," I said nothing, I just nodded my head while at the same time steadfastly thinking, *I believe the spaghetti was prepared al dente!* to avoid any chance that one day in confession a certain hard-nosed Father Huerta, who would doubtless have been *Beau Geste*'s Sergeant Markhoff's personal choice for Fort Zinderneuf's chaplain, would be reading me off as the most shameless and hardened chronic liar since Citizen Kane's biographer denied that in fact he'd said "Rosebud" *twice.* But then even with only my equivocating nod Jane exploded into smiles while tiny stars in her eyes danced a polka as she said to me, "*Yes,* Joey! *Yes!* You *trust!* You'll be *ready!*"

Which was as transparently clear to me then as a haiku written by Yogi Berra. I said, "Ready for what?"

She didn't say. And then abruptly from euphoria her face seemed to sag into a misty melancholy as she turned her head to look at herself in the mirror and, touching a hand to her hair, said softly and sadly, "I'm not pretty at all." Not knowing what to say except, "Hey, what are you, *nuts*?" I just stared at the perfection of her face for a bit and it was then that I noticed that except for the reddish hair she looked enough like Lourdes to be her sister. There was also this funny sort of marking on her cheek, the left one, and, "What's that?" I decided to ask her, pointing.

She shifted her eyes to me in the mirror.

"What's what?"

"That little circle with the X inside of it. It's on your cheek. You belong to some crazy-girl witch cult or something?"

"It's a birthmark, Joey. Like your smirk."

I looked up and saw the waiter hovering above us, distractedly picking at his wavy black mustache like he was feeling around for bits of chopped garlic that the chef had

reported missing. He also had an eye on the
door to the street as a couple with three little
kids came in after seeing the movie *Bambi*, I
guessed, as it was playing at the theater next
door and all of the kids were still blubbering
and sniffling, doubtless over the death of
Bambi's mother, who's shot by a hunter in
accord with Walt Disney's decision it was
time that they learned about the Problem of
Evil even if it messed up their psyches for life
and later led to them turning into serial
killers with their victims all members of the
NRA and always found with a note in block
letters pinned to their bodies saying:

THIS IS FOR BAMBI'S MOTHER, YOU FUCK!

The waiter looked down at us.
"Dessert? Profiteroles? Spumoni? Bisque
Tortoni?"
I ordered blueberry pie with chocolate ice
cream, something else I'd never had before
but which the Spirit of Tokay was insistent
that I order, to which Jane added spunkily,
"Make that two!" I eyed her as if I'd just met
her. *Gunga Din* with tears three times, I re-

flected, and blueberry pie with chocolate ice cream once, and it was then I got this pretty big crush on Jane Bent.

It was early October and one of those orangey full-moon nights, so we walked to the newly built East River walkway, just ambling along, with me at first undecided as to which way of walking would impress Jane more: Gary Cooper's suffering but stoic-faced "You'd Never Know My Indigestion's Killing Me" style or Humphrey Bogart's more intimidating lowered-shoulder slouch with a dead left arm held immobile across his waist like Duke Mantee in *The Petrified Forest*. Funny thing: as I was mentally trying out the styles, I think Jane pretty well understood what I was doing, because she'd glance at me sidewise with this knowing sort of fond little smile. The reflection of that pumpkin moon on the river and the string-of-pearl lights of the Brooklyn Bridge were so romantic that running through my head was the voice of Bing Crosby in a movie I'd seen where he's in a canoe on a moonlit night singing "Moonlight Becomes You" to Dorothy Lamour. But this being real life and not a movie I kept hoping that nothing would spoil the magic, like encountering a police truck fishing some derelict out of the river with these slender long poles with metal hooks on the end before slapping him into a wooden box with these loud squishy thumping sounds like the guy was a side of beef and even now still an all-around royal pain in the ass. This was something I'd seen that past summer when, walking down East 23rd the day before, some poor old bum came shambling past me in the opposite direction and I heard him saying, "Kill me, Jesus! Please! Please kill me!" over and over and without any trace of emotion, like he was praying the next day would be sunny so he could go to a Yankee game. I'd wondered if his was the body I'd seen fished from the river.

And if it was should I be sad or glad?

We sat on a bench for a while looking out at the river and the twinkling lights of the Brooklyn shore, not talking but refueling our souls while in the distance a tugboat hooted sadly along. Then I heard Jane asking me a question.

"Joey, do you pray?"

I turned and tried to read her. Her voice had been earnest and touched with concern, like her jade green stare now meeting mine.

I said, "What?"

"Do you pray?"

"Sure, I pray. I go to Mass every Sunday."

"I mean at night. Do you pray every night?"

I shook my head.

"You need to do it," she said. "It builds up graces."

"What do you mean?"

She was looking really serious now.

"The world's a battleground, Joey. I mean it. You can't see it, but we're really in a scary war with darkness, with these demonic evil shitheads, the 'Dominions' and the 'Powers' that Saint Paul goes on about, and inasmuch they've got most of the high-powered weapons we need to put on armor, which is grace, Joey, the grace of the sacraments; and a way we get to access that grace is by prayer." Then she added, "For a start."

"For a start?"

"For a start. Didn't your pop teach you night prayers, Joey?"

Well, I didn't know whether I should pull up my socks or sing "Swanee River," but wisely choosing neither I just gently shook my head. I mean, what could I say? Oh, well, sure: Pop had told me I should try to pray at night. He said that he'd promised my mom he would do that. But teaching me *how?* I mean, to get in the mood and teach me *right* Pop would have to be standing in deep meditation on a pointed crag about sixteen thousand feet in the air with the favored family eagles slowly flapping and circling all around him in the mist quietly cawing at him, *"Don't look down!"*

I didn't say this, of course. What I said was, "Not exactly."

"Come on then, kneel down and I'll show you."

My eyes bugged out a little. She was kneeling at the bench, her hands folded prayerfully on the wooden seat. "Come on," she said. "Do this for me, would you, Joey? It would make me very happy. Joey, *please?*"

Well, I did it. I knelt down beside her and

with a fervent prayer in mind, alright, which was that none of my classmates would happen by, but as it was Jane taught me a different one: "'Now I lay me down to sleep. I pray the Lord my soul to keep. If I should die before I wake, I pray the Lord my soul to take. Amen.' That's all you need to say," she told me. And then again that little sneaky caboose, "For now.

"But do it every night," she then added. *"Every night!"*

"Hey, you sweet-lookin' honey!"

Jane and I quickly stood up. It was a group of three guys, most likely eighth-graders from Our Lady of We Don't Need No Stinking Badges, one big and pretty brawny in a red tank T-shirt with the single word "SO?" on the front in huge letters. "Why don't you dump your skinny boyfriend," he went on, "and come along with us guys to a party? What do you say? You want to come? Sure, you do. Come on, I got something nice for you there. *Real* nice."

When I finally had to recognize the probability he was talking to Jane and not someone on the Planet Schwartz, before I could open my mouth to advise him his behavior was "not the way of Zen," the guy in the tank shirt reached to clutch at Jane's arm when suddenly, WHAMMO! She'd whipped around sideways and kicked him in the jewels, and with his mouth wide open in shock and awe, not to mention excruciating pain, Mister "I Am Not Zorro After All" slowly crumpled to the ground while the two lesser toughs held back, looking suddenly fearful and confused and not at all like Huntz Hall, a St. Stephen's grad who played one of the "Dead End Kids" in the movie. Meantime, Jane was now crouched in a fighting position with a tightly clenched fist held out in front of her and another fist coiled at her waist. *"Vamanos, hombres!"* she warned them. "I have power! I *am* the power!" Then she took a step forward and instantly the three *caballeros* turned and ran, heading back uptown, their disgraced fallen leader hobbling gamely as he straggled behind muttering threats of revenge that would have even made the Count of Monte Cristo blench, while now and then he would turn and shake a fist at us, yelling, "You going to see what going to hoppen to you now! You know? You going to see! My *God,* you going to see!" His Latino Jeremiads continued sporadically until, as he began to recede in the distance, a final valediction so faint that it might have been coming from the edge of the Andromeda galaxy dimly floated down to us from far upriver: "I feel sorry for you guys! You know? I'm feeling sorry so bad I'm going to *puke!!*"

The glow of the Tokay had worn off and I wasn't sure how I should take all of this. First my role as a provider and now this.

But I was quick to give praise.

"Holy whack!" I exclaimed. "Jane, where'd you learn judo?"

"It's not judo."

"Then what is it?"

"Effective. Listen, Joey, gotta go now. I got lots of stuff to do."

"Gee, so early?"

"Can't be helped."

"Well, okay then," I said. "I'll walk you home."

She shook her head.

"No. This is something I need to do alone."

"Such as what?"

"Seven churches," she said. "Okay? On Holy Thursday you get graces if you visit seven churches."

"It isn't Thursday, though. It's Friday."

She looked up at me with patience in her eyes. And something else. Maybe fondness. Maybe worry. Maybe both.

Looking aside, Jane folded her arms across her chest while a sigh fluttered down to the tabletop with the weight of a venial sin.

"Now it starts," she murmured.

She was shaking her head.

"Whaddya mean?" I said, frowning a little in puzzlement.

With this she turned back to me, her eyes a little tight as she answered, "You know perfectly well what I mean. Must you always be so quarrelsome, Joey? Do you have to be right every time? Someone tells you it's daytime, you insist it's night? Then they point to the sky and say, 'See, there's the sun,' and you give them your biggest killer line, 'Yes, *but!*' "

"What do you mean?" I said; "It really *is* Friday!"

"And you're stubborn as ever besides.

Now, listen, Joey, one more thing. It's important."

"*What's* important?"

"That it's okay to love me. But don't be *in* love with me. Okay? And be good to your father. He loves you so much." And with that she turned around and started quickly walking south while calling out to me, "*Trust,* Joey! The magic word is *trust!*"

Oh, yeah sure, I was thinking: Trust. I mean, who could you possibly believe about anything? The wiring in my brain was still shooting off sparks from that time near the end of third grade when Baloqui approached me, his eyes wide and his face an off-white, which was the best it could do whenever drained of blood, and grimly whispered in a horrified tone, "Oh, my *God,* Joey!"

"*What?!*"

"Oh, my *God*! I just found out what it is you have to do when you get married!"

"Yeah?"

"You have to put your weeney inside your wife's heine!"

I took a couple of steps backward, half yelling, half gasping at him, "*What?* Are you out of your *mind,* Baloqui? Get away from me! No! No, don't touch me! You *disgust* me! Where in hell'd you hear a crazy thing like *that?*"

"From a guy in fifth grade!"

I went numb. A fifth-grader! *This was authoritative!*

"Then I'm never getting married!" I gritted.

"Me too!"

We hugged tightly. I thought I heard a whimper.

The next month Baloqui's parents invited me to Thanksgiving dinner, which his family held the day after ours, and all through the meal I'd see Baloqui's dead stare go from his father to his mother and then back, and then he'd lower his head and mutely shake it.

I saw Jane take a right on a path that would lead her to Avenue A and then on to her Holy Thursday churches on a Friday. What a mystery she was: plucky as short, fat Tony Galento getting hammered in the ring by Joe Louis, and jumpy as fleas who've just gotten great news; dropping the F-bomb and then teaching me to pray; making sense, then being totally wingy. There was also this aura

about her, something spiritual; ethereal, really. And then I remembered some stuff that
she'd said to me, things like, "You're as stubborn as ever."

As *ever?* What did *that* mean?

5

Pop and I lived in this dingy little third-floor walkup at the corner of 31st Street and Second Avenue across from a raunchy new bar called the Health Club, where after my homework and my favorite radio shows, *Captain Midnight* and *The Shadow*, were done, I could tune in to some local and terrifically live free entertainment by leaning out the window to watch the nightly bar fights spilling out into the street, almost always involving a couple of old geezers in their thirties or forties—sometimes even lots older—and after they'd bloodied each other as much as their flabby, drunken swings ever could while their girlfriends or wives stood aside and kept moving their lips, saying, "Somebody stop this, would you? Stop them!" in a murmur so low even *I* couldn't hear it, and then the combatants would wind up with their arms around each other's shoulders and go back into the bar to buy each other a drink, the sound of music from a jukebox blasting out into the street as they opened the door, almost always Bing Crosby and "The Rose of Tralee" or "I'll Take You Home Again, Kathleen," and if Pop was standing anyplace where he could hear it he'd yell, "Joey, shutting window!" inasmuch as he was tired of the same old songs, but even probably more so, I'd have to suppose, because he'd come here as a child from Peru and had about much interest in "Galway Bay" as in hearing a duet of "I'm an Indian, Too" by Sitting Bull and Mohandas K. Gandhi. The songs might also have made Pop sad, as they probably made him think of my mom. Her name was Eileen. She was Irish. I'd never seen her. She died giving birth to me. Pop met her at Bingo Night in the basement of St. Rose of Lima Church when both of them lived in the Bronx. Pop had only one photo of her, one of those black-and-white jobs that had been taken of the two of them in Central Park and then slipped into a cardboard frame with SOMEWHERE IN THE U.S.A. at the top. Already blurry from the softness of the focus, the photo had yellowed and was badly faded so I could only make out that she was smiling and slim and had long wavy hair. I could barely even recognize Pop. Whenever I'd ask him to describe my mom he would always start to cry and then he'd go into the bathroom or he'd put on this black leather cap and go out into the street. I'd open a window, then, and watch him. I'd get worried if I saw him slowly walking toward the river.

I also stopped asking about her.

"Why so late, Joey? Almost ten o'clock. You want to eat?"

Wearing a torn old navy blue sweater and with skin that was the color of a waxed pine floor, Pop had sharp, strong features with very high cheekbones and an aquiline nose that knew who it was. You couldn't tell that he was over six feet tall because pushing those carts for all those years had curved his posture almost into a crouch.

"You looking funny," Pop told me.

"What do you mean? Funny how?"

"I don't know," he said, appraising me. "Different. Come on, now. You hungry? I fix you something good."

That was Pop. Concern about my care and well-being always coming ahead of any talk about discipline or who struck Juan. I thumped myself down into one of the two folding metal chairs set on opposite sides of this sad-looking, tan-colored plastic card table just off the kitchen where we'd eat all our meals and I'd also do homework. Pop had made enough money off his trade to upgrade our pitiful furnishings lately, but after Mom died I guess he mostly lost interest in everything but me. Our apartment had only one bedroom and Pop made me sleep there while he slept on the living room sofa.

"No, I ate, Pop," I told him.

"Ate what?"

I said, "Spaghetti and pie and ice cream."

I didn't think it was such a hot idea to mention the Tokay.

Pop wrinkled his brow.

"Spaghetti, Joey? Where? With the Pagli-arello family?"

My first thought was *Are you out of your mind?*

"No, Pop. A little restaurant on Four-teenth Street."

"Joey, where you get the money? I don't give you yet allowance for this week."

I said, "My friend paid, Pop."

"What friend?"

"A girl at school."

Pop came out of his crouch at this, stand-ing straight and tall for a second while his face was a gasp made flesh.

"You let *girl* pay for your food?"

"And a movie," I threw in before I knew what I was saying.

That did it, that was all the old man could take, and he launched into a rant about chiv-alry at first, and then the subject was "man-hood what is true and not fakey" and the real and proper order of things and how I'd sinned against the code of some Incas who always made the boys have to wait to have their hearts ripped out until after the girls

"Have you seen this pretty girl around?" I asked. "Jane Bent. Irish face with lots of freckles. Pigtails. Reddish hair. Eighth grade."

"Yeah, I might have," he said as he took a deep drag and looked off in pained thought as if agonizing over whether it was moral to throw his next bullfight in exchange for gang money he could use to send his epileptic brother to the healing waters at Lourdes in France. His lips curled inward in an O, he blew out an almost perfect smoke ring that he kept on staring at with pride as if he'd just built the freaking Eiffel Tower and was about to put the finishing touches on it. "I might have seen her at the movies," he finally allowed in this cryptic tone of voice.

I said, "You *might* have?"

He held up a hand. "Hold a second."

He waited for the smoke ring to dissipate completely, then turned to me with narrowed, searching eyes. "This girl," he said. "You're interested in her?"

"Why?"

"Because if it's the girl I have in mind she's a psycho."

"That's her!" I burst out with elation. "So

you know her! Do you know where she lives?"

"No, I don't and I wouldn't *want* to know."

"What are you talking about, Baloqui?"

"Who can say?"

"Who can *say,* you dumb spic? Who can *say?*"

"Alright, alright! I didn't see it myself. Someone told me."

"Told you *what?*"

Here Baloqui launched into a story so spectacularly stupid that at first I was sure he was pulling my leg. An eyewitness, he insisted—his thick, black eyebrows puckering together in keeping with the gravity of his message—had told him that Jane was seen levitating over a crowd at the refreshment counter at our beloved Superior cinema and had words with an usher before settling back down on the ground and running out into the street and out of sight. You could see he'd boned up on Poe because he ended with a spookily delivered "none knows whither."

I said, "You're kidding me, right?"

"Swear to God!"

"No, it's a joke."

"Well, not a funny one, then, is it?" he said pissily.

I wanted to shove needles into his eyes.

"This so-called eyewitness," I said. "Who was it?"

"It was Eddie Arrigo."

"Eddie Arrigo?" I echoed dully.

I couldn't believe my ears. Arrigo, after being left back three times, had finally gotten into a class graduation photo, all smiley in his blue serge confirmation suit, yet his legend lived on to benumb the normal mind and outshine things like cigarette ash and coal. At dismissal from class each day, when we would march in twos to the corner of Third Avenue, we would pass the all-glass second-floor front of a tarot card reader named Madame Monique, who in actual fact was Arrigo's mother and had once told Eddie, who then passed it on to us, that the twenty-seventh quatrain of the coded predictions of Nostradamus had been "seriously and widely as hell misconstrued" and that in truth it had to do with an alien "research" spaceship hidden inside the Goodyear blimp, though I suspected her interpretation of the quatrain had been seriously damaged, if not maimed, while in transport, inasmuch as Eddie had also once soberly reported that his mother's faithful spirit guide, "Irving," had told her that the Japs would attack Pearl Harbor— "a Hawaiian thing," as Irving had put it—on March 4, 1941, "April twentieth the latest!" So, okay, Captain Future of *Captain Future Comics* was always battling against the so-called "Yellow Peril," which was diplomatic code for Chinks and Japs and maybe even Samoans, for all we knew, but that wasn't supposed to happen until *1970*!

"Eddie *Arrigo*, Baloqui? *Arrigo?* What drugs are they insinuating into your sangria?"

Baloqui wouldn't look me in the eye. Instead, he flicked his cigarette butt into the street, then turned around and strode back into the library, as usual walking tall and with his chin tilted upward as if about to be awarded both ears and the tail while inwardly smoldering and thinking, "To hell with these mocking gringos who wouldn't know friendship from a used piñata!"

But he really had me going. Big.

I went back into the library, grabbed *Portrait of Jennie* off the shelves and took a seat at a reading table as far from Baloqui as I could, though he was still sitting facing me, slouched down low in his seat and with his black eyes shooting death rays at me from an inch above the top of the book he was holding propped open on the desk in front of him. I tried not to notice. *Good luck!* Every time I looked up from my book Baloqui's baleful stare would be on me like some vengeful Latino Banquo's ghost until I finally decided, *Screw you and your Thanksgiving turkey stuffed with fried green bananas and rice and beans!* I got up and slunk out into the street with glare wounds all over my face.

For a while I just paced back and forth out in front. I hadn't seen Baloqui in a sulk like this since I asked him for the answer to a puzzle that I'd read in the *Book of Knowledge*. "A brick weighs six pounds and half its own weight," I quoted, "and so what is the weight of the brick?" "That's a puzzle?" He'd scowled. "What does it weigh? It weighs nine pounds." "No, twelve," I told him, which might have been fine, but then I had to add,

"I got it right away." Well, we argued, and his bushy black eyebrows knitted together and at one point I thought he was going to deck me as his face was turning blue and he was shouting, "That's *ridiculous!* Your stupid book *lies!*" and then for days he would pretend not to see me or hear me until finally I retracted and said the *Book of Knowledge* answer had turned out to be a typo. I am not a hard man. So now I did a little thinking and decided that before messing up my friendship with the jerk, I should go to the Superior and fact-check Arrigo's story, which I did. I paid my nickel admission, walked into the lobby and found out from an usher that the theater manager, the guy I wanted to talk to, wouldn't be in until three, so while I waited with a nickel bag of popcorn in my lap I was able to watch a whole bunch of neat-o cartoons, and then a couple of cowboy chapters, one a Tom Mix and the other Buck Jones, in which hundreds of bullets were fired except no one ever seemed to get hit unless he was standing near Gabby Hayes, which of course made me wonder if Hayes was Italian and possibly related to the Pagliarellos. The first feature, in the meantime, was *The Great Dictator*, a Charlie Chaplin movie that had the packed crowd of us grammar school aesthetes constantly erupting in guffaws that were almost as loud as when someone in a movie went blind or was decapitated or had acid thrown in his face. Halfway through the Hitler-Mussolini barbershop scene, I checked the time on the Dick Tracy watch that I got for my birthday from Pop years before, and seeing it was ten minutes after three I got up and went out into the lobby, where I finally met up with the Superior's manager, a tall, stocky guy named Mr. Heinz. He was old, maybe twenty, twenty-one, and chewing gum with his mouth a little open and his hands on his hips as he stood staring down at me with this spazzed-out look in his eyes like he wasn't quite sure that he wanted to be conscious.

"So what's up, kid? You lookin' for a job? I'm real busy."

Right away I understood that I was going to have to grovel, but having so recently seen Gunga Din telling Victor McLaglen, "Din only poor beasty, Sahib" in a moment of breathtaking cinematic cringing destined never to be equaled, or even approached, until the sun grew cold and, long before that, the last executive at any TV or cable station running ads about erectile dysfunction and the state of one's colon at the family dinner hour, had been shot, disemboweled and given no rites, I knew exactly how to do it to perfection, which I'm sure Sister Joseph would have told me was just more evidence that "there *are* no coincidences with the Holy Ghost." And so after an "I know this sounds nutsy" preamble, along with a rich and heavy dose of "sirs," I repeated what Baloqui had said about Jane while at the same time telling Heinz that she was my sister who'd "been missing for days" and that any little clue "could be helpful to the police."

"The police? I haven't heard of any police coming by."

"Levitation's not a crime," I said.

"Probably not."

"But did it actually happen? Did you see it yourself, sir?"

He said, "No, kid. I didn't. And except for one person seems like no one that I talked

to about it did either. She was at the back
of this crowd at the candy counter. But one
of the ushers sure saw it."

"He *did?*"

"So he says. He said he yelled at her to
stop but she gave him 'the arm' and some
guff about a bell." Heinz shrugged. "I dunno."

I pointed to an usher coming out of the
theater.

"Is that him?"

"No, that's Louis. The guy you want to
talk to is Eddie."

"Eddie who?"

"Eddie Arrigo. He comes in at six o'clock.
You want to wait?"

"Oh, I'd like to, Mr. Heinz, sir. I'd like to.
But I've got an appointment with this grouchy
detective who's in charge of the search for
my sister. When I'm late he gets mad and
makes threats."

"He shouldn't do that."

"No."

I left and could hardly stand to wait until
Monday when I could get the straight skinny
from Jane herself, though I was scared she
might think me half a jerk for even bothering

to check out Arrigo's story, although, speaking of which, it might be time to put my cards on the table and confess that I was always into "out of this world" kinds of stuff and maybe more than a little too willing to believe, which of course will make a lot more sense to you after you consider that for maybe four months of second grade I believed that Doc Savage was an actual person, although, unlike Arrigo, and not wanting to be piling on or anything like that, I never claimed to be related to Doc Savage "by marriage." So okay, that's neither here nor wherever you want to put it, my only point being that when it came to reports of such things as levitation, my famed cynical smirk was nothing more than a cover as I tended toward *wanting* weird things to be true. As it happened my mask of superior snide was ripped off by Tommy Foley on one of those days where, always just before Christmas and Easter, my whole class would get marched into church two by two to sit in pews and wait in dread for our turn for confession because we never knew who'd wind up being our confessor, the wildly popular ninety-two-year-old Father Causey who had so heard it all and so endlessly often that if you told him that you'd murdered someone, he'd keep his head down and sigh, then say, "How many times?" and for your penance tell you, "Think about saying a Hail Mary," whereas the other priest was the previously mentioned Father Huerta, and we all would sweat bullets that he'd be our confessor after Paulie Farragher told us how when he'd confessed to him that in the past four months he'd had impure thoughts about girls "for sure once, maybe twice," Huerta growled, "Is that all you ever think about?" and gave him three decades of the rosary for a penance, which made me think Huerta was probably lucky to be in a state of grace and that the penitent's box was so small as I had this sudden vision of Farragher swinging his arms around in his patented windmill defense and maybe breaking Huerta's nose while he was giving absolution. So okay, it's now a Friday just before Easter when Foley, who is sitting beside me in a pew, leans over and whispers in my ear that he's heard from a source he refused to identify that if you

stare at the back of someone's head pretty
soon they'll feel the vibes and turn around
to see who's watching them, and he asks me
now to help him try it out, to which, of
course, I immediately agreed. I mean, it was
Foley who'd reported to me accurately that
if two or more people keep staring at somebody's shoes, like on a bus or the subway, at
first they turn their glances here and there,
trying hard to look oblivious and cool like
Noël Coward on opening night in London
with the V-2 rockets whistling close overhead and then exploding and shaking the
theater, when in fact they're really feeling
like the lead in some weirdo play by Franz
Kafka until finally they break and look
down at their shoes to find out what could
possibly be wrong with them. I admit that
we almost got beaten to a pulp one time on
the bus to the Central Park Zoo. We had to
pick on some guy wearing jackboots? Never
mind. Oh, well, sure, this is Gotham City
but not everyone gets rescued by Batman,
maybe only Father Causey and only if Batman is Catholic and thinks Causey and
Huerta are the only two priests in the city.

So anyway, I teamed up with Foley that Friday in church and we both aimed our laser-beam stares at the back of Winifred Brady's head when out of the corner of my eye I detected a strangeness, a long thin shadow that was swinging back and forth on the door to the tabernacle on the altar, and with my eyes opened wide in some excited, dumb schoolboy surmise, I poked Foley with an elbow and pointed at the shadow as I hissed at him in wonder, "Hey, Foley! Look at *that!*" An altar boy, Foley followed my point, and then he turned to look back at me with this oddly appraising and possibly borderline infuriating stare as he explained to me that while I had my head down fervidly praying that I'd get Causey, another priest had come out on the altar and had opened— and then a few seconds later closed—the tabernacle door and left the key in the lock so that the "occult" phenomenon I thought I was seeing was the shadow of the lazily swinging chain to which the key to the tabernacle door was attached.

"You thought that was something supernatural, El Bueno?"

It wasn't what he said, but that smile of bemused superiority that did it as I wanted to punch Foley in the mouth right then and there, but I was afraid I'd get Huerta for confession and he'd ask me if all I ever thought about was punching people. In the meantime, this "El Bueno and the Mysterious Swinging Shadow" episode turned out to be a blight on my reputation. Foley spread the word that not only did I break under water torture in the East 23rd Street public pool that past summer, but I would believe almost anything and had an incredulity threshold about thirty levels higher than Pope Leo III's when he met with Attila the Hun in the middle of a river and Attila explained to him his concept of "eminent domain." And then I made things worse, I guess, when egged on by envy of Timmy Lyons, who had held us all spellbound as he breathlessly told us that he'd had a dream of Christ in which the Lord had walked up to him and said, "Be a priest!" and then further, "When I woke up, I vomited," Lyons offered as vivid and multicolored proof that the dream was not a dream but a "visitation." My competitive nature aroused, I responded on the very next day with a made-up dream in which Christ not only said to me, "Joey, be a priest!" but as he said it he "put his hand on my shoulder and *squeezed*." I won the battle but lost the war, inasmuch as whereas Lyons was held in awe, who got the bad press for telling stories? Me. So I did a big turnaround. I couldn't take the giggling and the sly little smiles and began a campaign to become known as "El Bueno, the Ravager of Bullshit," which by now in seventh grade I had finally achieved.

It made me sad.

6

Right after my discussion with Mr. Heinz of Plato's *Phaedra* and its possible echoes in the Catholic existentialism of Gabriel Marcel, I wandered down to the East River walkway and sat on a bench just like any other kid who's been cow-kicked by a monkey for the very first time, only maybe just a little on the downcast side and hoping hard that maybe Jane would walk by. Instead, who comes along and plops his lank down beside me with a long-toothed, jagged grin and rigged out in full Boy Scout uniform with merit badges splashed all over this sash that he wore but the leader of my Scout Troop, "Upright" Olsen, which is what we all called him on account of him being so tall and with this honest open face and him always quoting stuff from the Boy Scout Oath about having to be "upright" and "morally strong," although anyone could see, just the same way I was looking at them now, these tiny numbers you could write on rice on both his thumbnails and all of his fingernails, which was how illegal "numbers takers" recorded their customers' bets so that if challenged by a cop they could quickly erase them with saliva and a handkerchief, the only difference between Olsen and any other numbers taker being Olsen seemed to favor forest green ink.

"Hey, how're they hangin', El Bueno?" he said with this twisted smile and pin-lights for eyes like Tommy Udo in *Kiss of Death* when he cackles, "I hate squealers' mothers," having just pushed an old woman in a wheelchair down a long flight of stairs to her death.

"What's up?" he went on. "You just takin' the air?"

"Pretty much, Mr. Olsen."

"Me too."

Which was a joke, as I knew he was probably on his way to some more of his numbers clientele, including maybe a stop to collect protection money from some poor old immigrant shopkeeper he'd previously bamboozled into thinking that he was in the Mafia.

"Didn't see you at the last three meetings. Sick or what?"

I didn't tell him the real reason. Every troop in the city took a nickel in dues but Olsen had upped it to a dime. Pop had already been stuck with the cost of my spiffy Scout uniform that he bought from this ultraexpensive Boy Scout Trading Post on Park Avenue and 32nd where there was always a security guard and with the clerks and the customers tiptoeing around on this thick plush carpeting and talking in barely a notch above a whisper so at first you thought you must have blacked out and somehow wound up in a wing of the Museum of Natural History where in these lit-up thick cases made of glass instead of caveman tools there'd be these hatchets and compasses and knives with the Boy Scout logo on them. I'd sometimes go in there and moose around with my nasally whistling, avid, warm breath condensing on the tops of the glass display cases as I ogled

stuff I knew I couldn't ever buy. I did notice
that neckerchiefs were very expensive.

"I had this bad cold," I told Olsen.

"For six weeks?"

"It was severe."

Olsen stared at me unblinking like some
cobra at a mongoose who's just told him,
"Hey, let's take a little break for a second,
okay?" and then he finally said, "Right" in
this quiet, dead tone and then stood up and
lurched off down the walkway with a "See
you next meeting." As he loped like some tall,
gimpy werewolf in his daytime form, I kept
staring at his wide-brimmed Boy Scout hat
and imagined the scene at his next "appointment," where he'd be holding out the Scout
hat upside down while collecting protection
money from the same Chinese laundry guys
we kids used to hassle, only this time with
a minor variation inasmuch as when Olsen
held up his hand with his fingers and thumb
splaying out, now the gesture meant "Pay
or Die on Friday." I often wondered if after
they'd paid him he gave them all merit badges
in lifesaving.

Spreading my arms out on the back of the

bench, I looked out across the river, wishing Foley were with me as I thought about a lot of those balmy summer nights when he and I would be glued to one of these benches watching bobby socks and saddle shoes slowly drifting by, or we'd be going through this booklet *Get Tough* that we'd chipped in to buy and was filled with these highly educational and, to Foley, deeply inspiring photos and sketches of British commandos breaking somebody's arm or his leg or maybe gouging out his eyes with their thumbs covered over in the same rubber caps that Miss Doyle always used when she'd be slowly turning pages in her ledger. We were acutely security conscious. Though we talked about other stuff too. Sometimes scary kinds of stuff. Like God. Like what if God hadn't created the worlds and there was absolutely nothing in existence, which discussions were always pretty short, I'll admit, since almost immediately at this thought our puny minds would short out and sort of gasp and want to throw up amid a shower of crackling electrical sparks like a couple of stymied head-hunters happening on the Tin Man in *The*

Wizard of Oz. Yet we still smelled the perfume when a really pretty girl walked by.

Pretty girls. There she was again. Right?

Jane Bent.

Head lowered, arms folded across my chest, I pondered the mystery enfolding Jane like an aura with ever-changing colors—on the one hand anxious for Monday to come when I'd be seeing her again and could get to the bottom of some things, and on the other already dreading the approaching end of the weekend and returning to the drabness of school, most especially with winter coming on when in the morning instead of walking five blocks in the freezing rain with cardboard in my shoes to plug the holes, I'd want to fake a bad cold so I could stay snug and warm in my bed while endlessly polishing my vast collection of secret decoder rings and badges and listening to grown-up radio serials like *Pretty Kitty Kelly* and *The Romance of Helen Trent*, although never *The Romance of Consuelo Chavez*, I noticed, or *Pretty Sandra Shapiro*. Only summer seemed livable to me then, and I even welcomed chubby old Sister Louise's constant warnings of the dreaded June

Regents exams in her husky, sandpaper voice, "In the merry month of June you'll be sweating," a threat she invariably personalized by always turning to glare at Bill Choirelli and adding a heartfelt "You fat tub of guts!"—which today might bring a lawsuit and find Sister Louise in an orange hood and jumpsuit doing the perp walk into some courthouse croaking loudly, "On the merry Day of Judgment all you ACLU scumbags will be sweating!" This followed by Foley, Baloqui and a few other bystanders quietly applauding and murmuring, "Hear, now! Hear! Hear, hear!" Foley idolized Sister Louise. Her position on torture would have never been in doubt.

Now my thoughts swirled back to Jane, this time to the puzzle of her cryptic words: *"It's okay to love me, Joey. But don't be in love with me."* What on earth could she possibly have meant? As I turned my head to the left and stared down the walkway with an ever-dwindling hope I'd see her walking toward me quickly with that moonrise smile and her arms held out to me, I saw someone quickly duck behind a group of strollers. It was Baloqui. Frimmled, I got up and started walking to the right, but when I turned and looked back I saw him stalking me again and then he jumped behind a tree to the left of the walkway. Grim-faced, I strode over to the tree and stood in front of it, arms akimbo as I growled, "You flaming refugee from a third-rate Toledo sword factory, why are you following me?"

"I'm not following," I heard Baloqui's voice answer hollowly.

"You were!" I said firmly.

"I was not. I was walking where you walked. Nothing more."

"Come on out from behind there!"

"No, they know me here now."

"You're standing behind a sapling! I can see you!"

"Touché."

Baloqui skulked around, looking grave.

"I am always your friend," he said somberly, "your most loyal, truest friend. But you are right. I lied. I have been following you."

"Why?"

"I guard."

I guard?

I'd been getting these déjà vu feelings lately and, looking back, I was having an unusually strong one because of this spook movie called *The Uninvited*, where Ruth Hussey and Ray Milland smell the scent of mimosa whenever a ghost named Carmel comes around, though in the end the ghost's good and she explains what she's been doing all this time, which is just those two words: "I guard."

But the movie wouldn't be made for another three years!

That was then. This is now.

But which is which?

"What do you mean, 'I guard,' " I said, and by now I was actually smelling mimosa as Baloqui said, "I seek to protect you," and then added his brand-new favorite coda, his increasingly annoying "Nothing more."

I looked over my shoulder as just for a second a suspicion sliced through my mind like a white-hot Damascus blade through Unguentine that Farragher and Connelly might be lurking in hiding and plotting to toss me into the river. I turned back and Baloqui put his hands on my shoulders, his intense black stare burning into mine as he said to me quietly and with emotion, "It doesn't matter what our parents might do with one another. No, with us there is a friendship that is strong and can never be broken. And so I guard, my friend Joey. I protect you."

"Protect me from *what?*" I blurted, exasperated.

"It's that girl, Jane Bent," he said. "Or whoever she *really* is."

That did it, that "whoever she *really* is," and I drew back and wrenched his hands off my shoulders. "What in freak are you talking about?!" I blustered, and then smoother than Evel Knievel sailing over a canyon on his favorite Harley with a sack full of gifts of appreciation for his longtime friends and contacts in the Las Vegas Hospital Emergency Room, Baloqui launched even higher into Bizarro Land with some lunatic story about Jane being spotted very late the night before standing next to a white limousine with the California license tag STARLET 1 and head-to-head in a "secret-looking, guarded conversation" with the *Little Orphan Annie* comic strip character and God-figure "Mr. Am!" Baloqui described him to a *tee*: "Very tall and with a pointy long white beard? Yellow cummerbund, black top hat and jacket? Come on, Joey! No question about it! It was him! And then that other guy, The Asp, he's in the driver's seat, okay? So they finish up talking, your girl and Mr. Am, and they get into the limo and drive off and what's spooky is you can't hear the sound of the engine. Now I'm not saying it really was them. Understand? I'm not saying it. If it really was them, then no problem: Mr. Am and the Asp, they're good people. But it actually *can't* be them, Joey! They're friggin' *cartoons!* So now what kind of people would *pretend* to be them? See what I'm saying? What kind of person would *do* that?"

Baloqui took a step back then, maybe to avoid a potential right cross, although actually I think it was more like in self-satisfaction as he folded his arms across his chest and nodded, saying, "Just looking after you, Joey. I don't know what they're after, but this girl is in it deep, she's in deep with bad people, plus it looks like they're rich, so they could finance expensive crazy plots to do you in. Stay away from her, Joey! That's the only thing I'm saying. Just look out!"

I blinked a few times to clear my head. I'd known Baloqui all the way from first grade and while he had a few crotchets— well, maybe more than a few—it wasn't until lately that I'd ever had reason to think that his brain waves, shall we say, had been inappropriately altered, and a paranoia dynamite fuse began sizzling and snaking through my mind about the people with the limo being rich, which made me flash on how Jane had whisked that five-dollar bill from her pocket. Who knew how many more might have been there? You know? Then my eyes began to narrow.

"You saw this yourself?"

"Joey, everyone sees things."

"True. But was it *you* who in fact saw *this?*"

"I have eyes."

"Yes, I *know* you have eyes. So do *I*. What I'm asking is are you the eyewitness to this, or is it somebody else with the initials F.A.?"

"And if it's me you won't believe it?" he suddenly blurted and—swear before God!—with a tremor in his voice and I could see he was scrunching up his eyes in a ludicrous try at manufacturing tears, or at least some mist, though I admit this pathetic but engaging bit of theater was surely no harder to take than his legendary "Pensive Stork" maneuver, although what followed, which was a choked-up "Okay for you, Joey!" was as close to a crushing final word as the set that I ran with could possibly use. And with this he whipped around, and with his hands in his pockets and his head bent low, he slouched away with this limp he was faking in a pitiful attempt at drawing my sympathy, and in my mind I could see him as Richard III grumbling, "Now is the winter of our discontent made even worse by this heartless prick El Bueno." I saw him suddenly stop and broadly smile as he seemed to have spotted something

on the walkway's grassy berm. He stooped
down to recover a thin piece of wood, but
then scowled and, tossing it away, gimped on.
He must have thought it was a "Lucky Stick."

7

I checked Dick Tracy, wondering how many locks he had picked with that icepick-pointed jaw, and I saw it was time to head home for dinner. Besides that my head hurt. Too much was going on inside of it, too many delirious, mysterious fandangos all bombarding my brain like it was some kind of run-down cargo spaceship being battered by swarms of pissed-off meteors because an article in *Science Magazine* had referred to them as "space debris." I took a last wistful look around for Jane and then started to wend my way droopily home, always watchful, of course, as the shadows of autumn gathered deeper, for a sudden Baloqui sneak attack.

Though as a matter of fact I was fond of the jerk. Being both Don Quixote *and* Sancho Panza, plus a touch of Trabb's Boy in Dickens's *Great Expectations* so relentlessly and quirkily deviling Pip, he had what most of us lack, which is vivid life, which I was practically certain beat vivid death, most especially when these scientists were constantly scaring us by insisting "vivid death" was where the universe was headed, though I suppose that when Miss Doyle heard the news, she said, "So?"

I chose an out-of-the-way route home that would take me past the "Supe" in the hope of maybe spotting Arrigo in the lobby and then somehow luring him out into the street, but, as it happened, when I got there he was standing out in front on a cigarette break. When he saw me coming toward him he froze for a second, his eyes wide and staring, then he flicked the cigarette into the street and tore back into the theater. Mr. Heinz was in the lobby at the time. He caught my eye, turned and stared at the auditorium door as it slowly and silently closed behind Arrigo, took another unreadable look at me and then lowered his head and shook it. So okay, so now I knew who was the real "eyewitness." But what on earth had ever happened to Arrigo? Three years before on Halloween night a whole bunch of us had stopped in at Boshnack's for a soda. Boshnack's radio was blasting and he said to us, "Shhhh, boys! Be quiet, now! Quiet! Listen!" Well, turns out it was Orson Welles with his famous phony "Martian Invasion" broadcast on CBS radio which he did so well it sounded like it really was happening and all these building-sized Martian spaceships had landed in New Jersey and were spewing out death rays left and right and all of us were shivering in our skivvies, that is, all except one of us kids who shook his head and dismissively flipped his hand, sneering, "Ah, come on, you guys! It's total bullshit!"

It was Eddie Arrigo.

• • •

Not to dwell on the matter, but in trying to sort out what had changed him, I would keep coming back to this one other time that we'd all come to Boshnack's on a sweltering summer night with the demon of boredom clawing at its cage within us. Many years later, when I was struggling for a living in Southern California, I lived for a time in a low-rent apartment complex in Studio City called the Valli Sands where there would be late-night Bing Crosby sightings when he would come to visit his future wife, Kathryn Grant, and where the tenant list ranged from Clint Eastwood—then under contract to Universal Pictures for a hundred a week and doing "wild tracks" of Indian war whoops and such for his pay—to me, then a midnight-to-dawn United Airlines reservations agent, and to the guy in the apartment next to mine who sold Bibles door to door and whose daily big meal was a budget-friendly serving of cabbage boiled in vinegar and lots of brown sugar, whereas mine was a dish of Uncle Ben's rice that I would cook in tomato sauce instead of water and then add sautéed onions and a lot of salt and pepper. It was a dish I would serve at the occasional little 'dos to which I would invite a few residents of the complex. Clint and Maggie, his wife, were at the first such gathering, sitting across from me on a tiny sofa, Clint with his hands clasped tightly around his knees and already beginning his *A Fistful of Dollars* persona of silent and inscrutable staring, although the look was benign and full of both wonder and a touch of bewilderment, perhaps, about what he was doing on the Universal lot the day that a studio executive pulled up to a Ventura Boulevard gas station where Eastwood was working as an attendant, took one look at him and offered him a studio contract. Clint had never given a thought to a career in movies. I learned this from Maggie. She spoke. Other than that it was a quiet affair.

But the next time, and times after that, were different as uninvited, struggling young actors showed up, including a young Jayne Mansfield, who was bubbly with a sweet-natured confidence in her future, and her husband, Paul, and their six-month-old baby. Of the three only Paul was quiet. He and Eastwood soon found each other and wound up in a staring contest over whose was the deeper silence. In the meantime, and finally getting to the point—because the crowds at these things were now straining my budget,

and not wanting to be outdone by the bur-
geoning attendance at the Brown Sugar Cabbage parties next door—after hours of nightly
experimentation, during which I would imagine myself to be Claude Raines in *The Invis-
ible Man*, dripping chemicals from vial to
vial, I found that mixing 7UP and sauterne
wine in a ratio of one-to-two will give you
champagne for about four minutes. The inspiration for this great humanitarian discov-
ery was an inevitable progression, I believe,
from that previously mentioned fascinating
night in July when the slender green bottle
of Vanti Papaya that we handed to Arrigo
was actually three parts Vanti and one part
collective youthful piss.

• • •

Arrigo took a sip or two, and then judged it
to be "a little bit off," so he handed it to
Boshnack who, after a test sip, shook his
head and agreed, "It's not right." It was soon
after that, is what I'm saying, that Arrigo
started making up incredible stories. Con-
nect the dots. I mean, I had to suspect it was
the atomically altered Vanti Papaya that had

somehow altered Eddie, although old man Boshnack had sipped at it too and the only bizarre effect it seemed to have was that the very next day he cut the price of chocolate Hooten bars from two to one cent and a Hooten with nuts from three to two. A little strange. Maybe Boshnack's immune system fought the thing off and he only got a touch since the price of egg creams stayed the same. But then who knows? It could even be that Eddie found out what we'd done and was slyly and secretly eating his cookies as he showed us that revenge is a dish best served not only cold but maybe endlessly as well.

Right after my encounter with Arrigo at the Supe, I doubled back to Second Avenue and as I passed the Chinese laundry who do I see but "Upright" Olsen in what looked like a pretty heavy argument with one of the laundrymen, probably the owner, and then two others came out from the back and were yammering and mad as hell and right away I saw another of my front-page headlines:

DEAD SCOUTMASTER FISHED FROM RIVER
FLATIRON-SHAPED BURN MARKS ON BODY

And below it the subhead:

**Scout Hat Filled with Cash Found Floating
Upside Down. Cops: "Suicide Ruled Out"**

I hurried on before Olsen could turn and see me and then afterward say the whole thing was all my fault because if I hadn't missed the last three meetings he wouldn't have had to transfer his annoyance with me to the Chinks by raising their protection fee from 7 to 10 percent.

You can prove almost anything you want if you want to.

• • •

Pop had cooked Peruvian shish kekab for dinner with a side of corn and boiled potatoes, and as we ate, our little curve-topped Philco radio was booming out the Saturday shows that began at five o'clock with *Kay Kyser's Kollege of Musical Knowledge* ("Make way for Her Nibs, Miss Georgia Gibbs!"), and then Bob Hope, Fred Allen and *The Hit Parade*, which played the top fifteen songs of the week; and, of course, *The*

Lone Ranger, which in every single show
had the Masked Man declare to some bad-
ass, "You're not hurt! I only shot the gun
out of your hand!" What I achingly longed
for was right after that to just once hear a
moan and the thud of a body falling to the
ground. Pop loved *The Lone Ranger*, and
the *Red Skelton Show* even more because
of Skelton's running character "The Mean
Widdle Kid" who every week made Pop
smile and chuckle with delight at his "If I
do, I get a whippin'," and then after a pause
for wicked thought, "I *dood* it!" Pop was so
pleased that I could imitate the voice of the
kid to a tee and at random times he'd smile
and say, "Joey, doing for me now 'I dood
it!'" It tickled him so! And when I'd done it
he'd look down and shake his head and start
to chuckle just the way he always did at the
name "Baby Snooks" or the voice of his favorite newscaster, Gabriel Heatter. Imitating
radio voices was the reason I was popular
in school, though later on in my high school
years when I discovered I could do a really
chilling movie werewolf cry, it was a whole
other opposite story inasmuch as not anyone,

not even Pop, would ever dream of saying, "Joey, doing for me now scary werewolf call," most especially on a Sunday in Central Park while we're watching all these honking, ungrateful seals being fed and complaining like they'd just been harpooned when a fish didn't score a perfect strike into their mouths as if the City could afford to hire Whitlow Wyatt, the Brooklyn Dodgers star pitcher, to come down there every day at two o'clock to throw flounder straight into the mouths of a bunch of glistening, spoiled little shits.

"What you do today, Joey?"

I shook my head as I chewed and swallowed, and then finally answered Pop, "Not much."

"Me too."

Yeah, sure: just busting his hump with that hot dog cart.

I thought of Jane:

"Be good to your father. He loves you so much."

How could she know such a thing? Were her mom and dad friends with the Pagliarellos? Or was it just a pretty easy guess?

"Something wrong, Joey?"

"What do you mean, Pop?"

"You face. You thinking hard about something."

I stabbed at the potato with my fork.

"No, nothing, Pop. Really. Just regular."

"Could be this girl who buys spaghetti for you, Joey?"

"Ah, come on, Pop! I'm okay! I mean, really! I'm fine!"

Pop kept studying me, chewing on the stem of his briar pipe. He wasn't buying it and I knew it. I was thinking about scads of things: Jane Bent and Mr. Am and the Asp and Baloqui, plus this sense of unreality that would drop over me at times like a Faraday cage reconfigured to block out time, and now and then I would feel, however distantly and through a veil all too freaking darkly, that *events were repeating themselves!* Not just moments, but in blocks of months— even years! It wasn't déjà vu, it was déjà *everything!* At times I even knew what was coming next! Very rarely. But like now. The radio. The *Hit Parade*. A new "bonus song" about the Lone Ranger:

Gimme those reins, there's pep in my veins.
Onward westward ho! Hi-yo Silver, Hi-yo!

I knew the words before I heard them!

"Come on, you thinking very hard, Joey. Tell me what about."

I said, "Homework, Pop."

What should I have said? I see the future? There are lies that don't exactly rend the fabric of the universe.

Pop got up and cleared his plate, then came back to the table with a bottle of Schlitz, his favorite beer. He liked its faintly salty taste. I kept eating and he kept on studying me thoughtfully. Meantime, the *Hit Parade* was still going and now after "Hi-Yo Silver, Hi-Yo" came "The Three Little Fishies":

Boop boop dittum dattum wattum, choo
Boop boop dittum dattum wattum, choo

Pop turned a blank look to the radio.

Number 3 on the *Hit Parade*.

I heard a rumble of thunder and then a burst of heavy rain sloshing down against the window panes so loud that you couldn't hear the song, an event that I'm certain St. Thomas Aquinas would have cited as a "Sixth Way" of proving God's existence. I started to brood about how maybe this was some kind of warning that we ought to start thinking about building an ark in case the "Hut Sut Song" ended up at Number 1:

Hut-Sut Rawlson on the rillerah
And a brawla brawla sooit

I said, "Pop, do you pray?"

He was hoisting the Schlitz to his lips when he stopped and looked across the little table at me. "Do I pray? What kind question, Joey? Yes. Yes, I pray. Not with words. With my heart. Be always good to people, Joey. That is prayer." Looking aside, I just nodded and said quietly, "Right." Pop was big and very strong and there'd been times when he'd prayed with his fists, but I didn't think it was such a hot idea just then to mention it or how he once broke a would-be mugger's arm and then another time the nose of some high school football hero talking trash to a little old lady on account of she'd told him to shut his mouth when he'd called out to a girl in the rumble seat of a car that was stopped at a traffic light, "Hey, you wanna screw?" If I'd asked him what maiming had to do with kindness, I knew he'd just tell me that of all his humanitarian acts these two were possibly the kindest of all inasmuch as, "From now on they be good, Joey. Right?" He took a swig of the beer and then looked me in the eye. "Something wrong, Joey. Tell me. Tell your father." Which is when my unconscious mind must have decided to run to the front of the bus, grab the driver by the shoulders and shake him awake.

"*Be good to your father, Joey.*"

The setup couldn't have been better.

I put on a hangdog face and looked aside.

"Ah, it's nothin', Pop. Really."

"No, is something, Joey. Tell."

I shook my head and murmured, "No, Pop. No. It's so selfish."

"I not care. It's alright, Joey. Tell. I give you anything."

"Pop, you've given me enough, so just forget it. Okay?"

"No, not okay. I want to know. Now I worry."

I looked up into his big chestnut eyes. He was scared.

"Oh, no, Pop! I don't want you to worry!"

"Then must tell me, Joey! Tell!"

"You won't get mad?"

"No-no-no, Joey! No!"

"Ah, geez! I just hate myself for asking!"

"Asking *what*, for God's sake?"

"I need a favor, Pop."

"A favor? Dot's all?"

"It's something big and that's all I'm going to say."

Pop buried his face into arms that he'd folded on top of the table and, utterly exasperated, said nothing. A sigh got lost in the wool of his sweater.

"Sheesh, Pop, if it means all that much to you!"

"I waiting," came the muffled and hopeless murmur.

"I want to sleep in the living room. There. I've said it."

For a couple of seconds Pop didn't stir, but then he looked up, his wide brow furrowed

with incomprehension as he suddenly exploded, *"What?"*

"See? I knew you'd get mad, Pop! I knew
it!"

"No, not mad! Only not understanding,
Joey! Why?"

I said, "The fights."

And then I launched into a story that
would have made even the most hardened
white tiles in our bathroom, which had seen
about everything, weep as I spoke of the
loneliness of the long-distance bedroom
sleeper, and how I'd be scared by "funny
noises," like these creaks and little spooky
tap-tap-taps in the ceiling, and most times I
couldn't sleep on account of I'd be thinking
so hard about the Health Club fights I was
missing, not to mention having windows
that didn't look out to darkness but out to
the street and familiar sounds: cars passing,
punches and curses—anything but *tap-tap-
tap!* All a steaming heap of cow-flop, of
course, but there was no other way to give
Pop what he needed and deserved: a real bed
with a downy mattress.

"Do not cry, Joey. Please."

I rubbed a knuckle at the corner of my eye.

"I won't."

"Couch not comfortable, Joey."

"Not for me, Pop. I'm smaller," I told him.

Well, he studied me for quite a little while until he turned toward the faint sound of jukebox music as someone either entered or left the Health Club. Then he turned back to me and said, "Okay."

"Oh, *thanks,* Pop! *Thanks!* Oh, *wow!*"

I did everything but slobber and kiss Pop's hand.

He still seemed to be thoughtfully appraising me.

"You go out tonight, Joey?"

I said, "No, Pop. Too much rain. I'll do homework."

Sister Joseph had assigned us to write fifteen hundred words on the topic "Why St. Francis of Assisi Talked to Birds but Not Fish."

"Try to make it original," she'd said.

Pipe stem in his teeth, Pop nodded and said, "Good boy."

I went back to my dinner feeling happy as Larry. Pop got up with his beer and walked over to a window where he stood and looked out at a fall of rain so heavy it seemed almost on the verge of violence. "Tonight they fight inside," he said quietly. "Too bad." Then he turned to me and smiled mysteriously and in a flash I saw the painting and the caption:

Peruvian Male Mona Lisa with Beer

These were mists I couldn't penetrate.
Ever.
Later that night while still doing my homework—I had narrowed the saint's disinterest in fish, by now, to a single species: carp—Pop came out of the bedroom in his pajamas, gave me a hug and then went back inside and closed the door. A second later he opened it a crack and said, "Joey?"

"Yeah, Pop?"

"There is woman at school she really having green hair?"

"Where'd you hear that?"

"Then is true?"

"Yeah, it's true. Pop, who told you about that?"

He said, "Tony. Tony Pagliarello. What her name, Joey?"

"Doyle, Pop. Her name is Miss Doyle."

"I want to meet her."

What was this?

I said, "Why?"

He wasn't looking at me now, he was staring just over my shoulder with this faraway look in his eyes. I couldn't tell what it was. Maybe sadness? Fond remembrance? Both?

He said softly, "Tony say to me she crazy."

Then he mutely turned away and closed the door.

I slept on the living room sofa that night and it wasn't that bad except I dreamed I was deep in the Amazon jungle desperately searching for something important even though I had no clue as to what it might be or what these Hari Krishna bozos were doing there cavorting and dancing in a circle all around me while they're shaking and slapping at their tambourines while chanting over and over again, "What a schmuck!"

Never mind. I slept deeply and oh so well.

I woke up to church bells ringing. Not St. Stephen's, though. Farther off. I sat up and scratched at my chest through my red-and-white striped pajamas while I looked out the window and could see that it was still coming down in buckets. Big stretch. Big yawn. No sound from the bedroom. Pop must have still been asleep and dreaming that he'd died and gone to heaven. I got up and was padding toward the kitchen for some juice when I happened to look down through a window to the street across the way and saw a woman in a fisherman's yellow raincoat and hat standing holding an umbrella. She was staring up at the window and when I stopped and stared back she started happily and excitedly smiling and waving to me. Then my heart jumped a little because she sort of resembled Jane, I thought. But then I saw she was older, in fact a *lot* older. She quit waving and blew me a kiss.

"Joey?"

I turned my head. Pop had cracked open the bedroom door. He was looking kind of down. Almost cranky.

"Yeah, Pop?"

He shook his head, looking even more troubled.

"I am sorry, Joey, very, very sorry, but I cannot sleep in bedroom. I cannot. I do not know what is cause. Maybe noises like you say. I do not know, Joey. Habit, maybe. Something. I have to sleep again on couch. That's alright? Maybe now you should be always leaving bedroom door open. When they fighting very loud you still be able to hear. It's okay, Joey? Sorry. Very sorry."

"Yeah, that's fine, Pop. No problem."

"I know."

So what was *that*?

I watched him peering out at me as he slowly closed the bedroom door, and then I turned to look down at the woman below on the street. But she was gone. Vanished. Not in evidence. I even opened the window and leaned out into the rain, looking this way and that, but there wasn't any trace of her. Drenched, I shut the window and went on into the kitchen where I poured myself a glass of orange juice and then stood with my back to the icebox, sipping and thinking about the woman blowing me a kiss. There were lots of crazy people in Gotham. Two days before there was a girl walking past me on Second Avenue shouting "Government!" over and over at the top of her voice and not sounding all that terribly pleased. My mind went to Pop and the sleeping arrangements, and, *Oh, well, I tried,* I thought. *I tried. At least that was something.* But then as I was lifting the juice to my mouth again, all of a sudden I stopped as I remembered something: Was that a sly smile that I'd seen on Pop's face when I was watching him close the bedroom door? Now I heard the grinding of a faucet handle being turned and then water running hard in a bathroom sink, and looking off I smiled faintly and nodded as, "Oh, yeah," I softly murmured. "Oh, yeah."

Peruvians. Who among them could you possibly trust?

8

I guess the title of a movie about the next day would be *The Lady Vanishes*. Most Sundays after twelve o'clock Mass I'd tote grocery bags for tips at the market, but the stupid heavy rain and fierce wind never stopped, as if some Hollywood studio had arranged it to coincide with the release of *The Hurricane,* a South Seas Jon Hall starrer, so I sat around at home with a three-inch paper scissor cutting out a Barney Google mask from the *Journal-American* Sunday funnies, thus setting up the reason that at the end of my life my tombstone should be totally blank but for the single word in tall block letters, DUPE! for I'd followed the paper's instructions that by "thoroughy mixing" flour and water I would wind up with glue. The lying fucks! I also entered a couple of their fraudulent puzzle contests. "Neatness counts!" they always said. Yeah, sure. Well, I gave the right answers to all of the questions in all of the puzzles all of the time, and as for neatness my answers were in perfect block letters, I'd even dust them for flyspecks, for crimminey sakes! But do you think I ever won? Not once! I tried everything, even setting down my answers on paper that I'd cut into the different geometric shapes of the most popular and bestselling bars of soap, and at the end, in humiliating desperation, a bleeding, humongous heart on the back of which I wrote in neat letters, IT FLOATS. Yes. Memories are made of this.

• • •

Monday morning Jane wasn't in school. Bummer. I had so many things to ask her. Come lunchtime I tried to console myself, trudging despondently to Lexington Avenue and 27th where the publishers of Superman comics were ensconced and I wound

up talking to some girl in reception and doing my ever so insouciantly charming and
engagingly innocent altar boy act while underneath I was seething and basically asking
where in freak was the Superman badge I'd
written in for, a demand I finished off with
hooded lids and a barely audible, "Neatness
counts." The girl gave me a pretty odd look
at that but then must have decided that she
hadn't really heard it since not only did she
give me the badge but a Superman Club decoder ring as well!

Some Mondays don't have to be all that
bad.

But by Friday things were rotten: still no
Jane.

"Hey, you seen Jane Bent anywhere?"

The eighth-grader in the school yard, a
truck-sized brute named Leo Zalewski, put
down the ruler whose end he had placed
against a loose upper molar. He'd been about
to bang it hard with the butt of his fist, this
being our version of "affordable dentistry."
Leo's eyes were always moist but now as he
looked down at me they seemed on the verge

of drowning. "Joey, thanks," he said. "Thanks a lot."

"What for?"

"I was about to bash out the wrong tooth."

"Geez, I'm glad I just happened along."

"Some coincidence, huh?"

I said, "Yeah."

I'd decided not to mention the Holy Ghost.

"So whaddya want?" he asked me.

"Have you seen Jane Bent?" I repeated.

"Seen *who?*"

"Jane Bent."

"Who's she?"

"Who's *she?*"

My response not having advanced the state of either his knowledge or undoubted deep interest in who should be favored in the Joe Louis–Billy Conn heavyweight boxing match that night, Zalewski looked bored and turned away. "Gotta find myself a mirror," he mumbled. He'd started walking toward a door to the school and the basement boy's room that was constantly redolent of urine and chalk, turning briefly to wave and stare at me wetly as he uttered, "I'll never forget you, pal."

I went and collared another eighth-grader that I knew, Billy Burns. "Hey, what's up?" he said, unwrapping a penny Hooten bar.

"Listen, Burnsy, have you heard why Jane Bent's not in school? What's the story? Is she sick? What's goin' on?"

"Jane who?"

"Jane Bent."

"Never heard of her."

"Whaddya *mean?*" I said. "Jane! Jane Bent! She's in your class!"

"Since when?"

"Are you *nuts?*"

"Are *you?*"

It could be that I was. I went on to ask other eighth-graders, but every one of them told the same story. I mean, talk about *Gaslight*! I'd seen her in the school yard! She'd been here! This was some kind of crazy mistake, I was thinking, like these guys must have misheard her name. And then the bell rang out in the school yard and we all trooped back to our classrooms, me being the only one walking like a zombie. Before the second bell for the start of class, Sister Louise was preoccupied with searching for something in this big black satchel of hers on her desk and I could pretty well guess what it was. Different nuns had different variations on torture. Sister Marguerite's, for example, was mental and perhaps the most fiendish of all. We would scribble away, writing compositions, which after you had finished it you'd take to her desk and hand it to her and then stand there watching her read it, and when she'd finished she wouldn't look at you, she'd just turn away with this quiet moan like she was getting warmed up to spend a couple of weeks in the Garden of Gethsemane as she placed your paper atop the stack on her desk and then quietly said to you, her expression inscrutable, "Thank you. You may go back to your seat," and then you'd hear this pained sigh from behind you. But then sometimes, when one of the brighter kids handed in a paper, she would dredge up a tight little weary smile and say with her thick Irish brogue, "Ah, well, now maybe *here's* something sure to brush away

the cobwebs from my heart," and she'd read
it and then slowly turn away with that same
dead, unreadable expression as she word-
lessly placed your composition on top of the
others, after which she'd prop her elbows
on her desk, lower her face into her hands
and then slowly shake her head. Equally effective, though far less inhumane, was the
special weapon that Sister Louise was now
groping to find in her bag, her dreaded nail-
studded "Guidance Ruler," and seizing the
chance while she was distracted, I grabbed
hold of Paulie Farragher and asked him in
urgent whispers to confirm that he'd actually
seen and met Jane.

"Jane who?" he hissed back at me.

"Bent! Jane Bent! Pretty girl with pigtails?
Came over and shook your hand and said,
'Nice' when you'd finished up a fight in the
yard?"

"Who told you that?" he hissed.

I gurgled, *"You!"*

Sister Louise looked up, half amazed and
half not gruntled. "What is it, El Bueno?" she
husked in her gravelly Lionel Stander voice.

"Nothing, Sister. Some kind of bug just landed on my neck."

"So instead of slapping at it you decided just to accuse it?"

I hadn't thought fast enough. She'd been as likely to swallow my story as to take off her hood and then fill it with drugged Brazil nuts to feed to the pigeons camping out on our window ledges, cooing and strutting around like they thought they were really special and the white stuff all over the ledges was tributes from subservient finches, but she hadn't found her weapon as yet, so she lowered her glare to her briefcase in what I would describe as extreme slow motion, maybe thirty-six frames per second, and possibly wishing that she were the Medusa. She ended it all with a "Hmph!"

At mid-morning recess I landed on Farragher again until at least he said *maybe* he remembered Jane. "Yeah, some girl shook my hand," he allowed, but then he had to add "Maybe," explaining that his windmill defense could at times cause "some dizziness" in the "aftermath of battle."

"Where'd you learn that word?" I said, my blood running hot.

"What word?"

"The word 'aftermath,' you moron!"

Many hands at last disengaged mine from his throat.

For now.

At recess I collared Baloqui, grabbing him forcefully by the front of his sweater and pulling him close to ask, my eyes wide, my nostrils flaring, "Listen, tell me, is there really a Jane Bent at this school?" And after his usual trademark frowns and glares of intently probing paranoid suspicion, not to mention his infuriating quietly uttered demand to know, "Why is this important to you?" he confirmed to me that Jane *was* enrolled at St. Stephen's and confided in a whisper behind his hand that the boys in eighth grade were just having me on. But then what did *that* mean inasmuch as he had previously confirmed the existence of the Asp and Mr. Am, and, if pressed, would have sworn that not only was Nancy Drew a real person but she would "probably be coming to Thanksgiving dinner."

"Come on in, El Bueno. Take a seat."

There was no other way.

Miss Doyle motioned to a chair beside her desk where she was probably bringing my tardy record up to date by inscribing an infinity symbol in the box headed "Number of Times."

"Be with you in a minute," she said.

I sat down. Through the glass partition of the file room I saw Sister Veronica's hood bobbing up and down and out of sight a few times very quickly in succession like some huge cloistered blackbird high on amphetamines and thinking that worms could be found in file drawers. On Doyle's desk I saw a Glidden's Paint color chart with the odds pretty even she was making a selection for either her apartment kitchen or her hair. I was also surprised to see a little framed photo of Clark Gable on her desk behind a clutch of white daisies in a water glass half filled with water. I was strangely touched. I could hear Judy Garland singing "You Made Me Love You" and wondered whether Doyle wrote "Dear Mr. Gable" letters in her mind. Finally, she lifted her pen from the ledger, and as she swiveled around to warily appraise me, the humongous cross that always dangled at her chest made a soft bumping sound against the edge of the desk. "So what's up, El Bueno?" she asked me. "You got a new mask to show off or am I looking at it right now?"

I said, "No, ma'am. No mask. I'm all me."

This didn't seem to relax her.

"And then?" she said.

"And then what, please, ma'am?"

Doyle squinted suspiciously. "What do you want?"

I want nothing but the best for all of mankind, came to mind as a way of sort of easing into things, but in the presence of Miss Doyle's overwhelming emanations of greatness, all I could think of was to blurt out, "My dad would really really like to meet you."

She looked at me blankly for a moment, then said, "Why?"

Oh, well, what to say *now* for cripessakes! "I don't know" was a total loser, and "Because he thinks you're crazy," I imagined, doubtless worse. But then my basic feral cunning returned to coat my honeyed, lying tongue with moonbeams:

"Oh, I talk about you almost all the *time!*" I gushed.

"You do?"

"Oh, yes, truly, Miss Doyle! I do!"

Her eyes narrowed.

Looking back, I think the error was the "truly."

"Okay, let's have it, El Bueno. What's really on your mind?"

"Jane Bent, ma'am."

"Who?"

"Ah, come on. Jane Bent. You see, her birthday's coming up next week and I wanted to send her a birthday card and maybe a couple of"—my eyes flicked to the daisies on the desk and then back—"well, daisies. Just a random choice. But I don't know her address and she hasn't been in class all week so I . . ."

"Okay, hold it, kid, hold it," Doyle told me as she lifted up a hand palm outward. "You say her name's Jane B-e-n-t, Bent?"

"Yes, that's right," I said. "The one in eighth grade—I mean, just in case there's two of them."

"Just in case there's two of them," Doyle echoed dully.

She leaned back in her chair and folded her arms.

"Is this another of your put-ons, El Bueno?"

"Put-ons?"

I was frowning in puzzlement, my expression more pious than Frank Morgan's as the Old Pirate in *Tortilla Flat* when he asks his dogs about a vision of St. Francis of Assisi in the woods: *"Did you see him, boys? Did you see him?"*

"Yeah, put-ons. Like the time you called a limousine service to come pick up Sister Veronica and take her to a prom at the Hotel Edison."

"You're seriously telling me I did that?"

Inclining her head a little, Doyle seemed to be appraising me with a distant, guarded fondness. It was as if she were discerning a kindred spirit.

"Is your father anything like you?" she asked me.

"Ma'am?"

She didn't answer. She just swiveled around, picked up her pen and went back to work. "Someone else would kick your butt for this, El Bueno. Of course we both know that there's no Jane Bent at this school, much less two of them, for God's sake!" She shook her head. "Why do you do these things, would you tell me?" Then she sighed and murmured something very softly.

It sounded like, "It must be in your blood."

9

Maybe there's more to the eye than meets it. Were Jane and Nurse Bloor and the universe real, or was I trapped in a virtual reality video game being played by some snaggle-toothed, teenaged alien being with acne, vast powers and a history of extended bouts of narcoleptic blackouts? So one second I'm sitting in Doyle's office and the next it's roughly seven months later with me on the Cyclone, a roller-coaster ride at Coney Island, as we're starting down the first big vertical drop with my stomach going weightless and me yelling my head off in the middle of May. I'm not saying that I "time tripped," you know, like Billy Pilgrim in *Slaughterhouse Five*, although it also wasn't Rip Van Winkle being wakened from a sleep of two hundred years by the roar of a 747 flying low overhead and him shaking his fist at the sky while cursing Mendel and "every other lame-brained, dipshit geneticist" who might have collaborated in the breeding of mosquitoes to such a titanic size and shouting hoarsely at the jet plane's contrails, "What's the goddamn *good* of it, man, would you tell me?" I not only knew that time had passed but also *how* it had passed: that it was almost summer, and that the Japs had bombed Pearl Harbor and Jane was still vanished from the face of the earth. Yes, I knew these things, but not as I would have if I'd actually *lived* them.

It was more like a movie I'd seen.

The mighty Cyclone clattered to a gradual stop. I got off and started glancing all around me furtively and probably with big white eyeballs rolling around like Peter Lorre being hunted by the mob in *M*, which of course was not *exactly* my situation, although the way I used to look at things then it was close. It seems Sister Louise, in her bountiful view that even morons and future

wanted criminals like us should have some
modicum of mercy and reward against the
chance that, as the dreaded statewide Regents
Exams approached, we might suddenly rebel
and start nailing heretical and scurrilous
theses to the massive St. Stephen's Church's
doors reading:

Who Is to Say When a Sin Is Mortal?

So a few weeks before, and in her usual
froggy voice, the good sister had decreed
for us a "stately pleasure dome" by which
she could have meant a cool and quiet pond
with giant lily pads floating on its glassy
surface, although in fact she meant our class
would have a school day spent instead at
Coney Island, which was great, but then
each of us boys was to pair off with one of
the girls for the day and pay their way for
all the rides. Yes. Getting to Know Me. We
got paired up in a raffle of sorts, picking
numbers out of a box, but instead of a regular number, instead I got the dreaded *Trea-*

sure Island "black spot," the notoriously gloomy Vera Virago. But never mind. No biggie. Okay? And I was totally with the program until we got to Coney and I sniffed that sea air and the sweet smell of taffy enfolded in that rich, wet aroma of those crinkled and salted potato fries and grilled hot dogs with mustard and relish from Nathan's, which is when Satan swooped down and grabbed me, then took me to the top of the Parachute Jump, where he sweepingly gestured at the goodies below while at the same time cupping his hand against my ear as he whispered, "All these and lots more do I offer you, Joey! Dump Virago and double your well-deserved pleasure! Didn't you toil and slave toting bags for old ladies for that dollar and eighty cents that you've saved, sometimes pissing in your corduroy knickers from depression at even having to talk to them, to answer their dithering questions while your urinary tract was close to bursting and requiring every bit of concentration on your part to prevent you from soiling? No, Joey, there is no free lunch, none at all, and most especially not for Vera Virago.

Remember how mockingly she laughed when you fell playing touch tag in the school yard, badly skinning both your knees on the pavement? There was blood, a *lot* of blood, I recall. You know, I doubted my eyes when I saw—or at least I *think* I saw—well, on top of your hurt she was flipping you 'The Bird.' Look, I shouldn't have said that. Okay? Just forget it. I mean, who knows what I actually saw. Matter of fact I've got an eye exam coming up soon for new reading glasses, so there's at least a 5, maybe 10 percent chance I was mistaken. She could even have been signaling someone; you know, someone in her club, perhaps some secret sign of friendship between them. And then who knows what 'The Bird' sign means in Albania, Joey, or to the Huaorani tribes of the Amazon. Okay? Let's not buy trouble. Oh, well, yes, yes, I know; I know her whole pathetic story: how she's suffered from severe depression and is so deeply and neurotically insecure that if it isn't taken care of by the time she's twenty-one she'll go to bars and then slip herself a date-rape drug. Is that really your concern, Joey? Really? I don't think so. Meantime, look, Joey! Look! Look down at Nathan's! Fresh fries are coming out, all ready for Total Catsup Immersion! Think how many you could eat without having to share with that totally vicious, un-scrupulous bitch who only yesterday . . . No. No, forget it. I'm sorry. No, really. I mean it. I misspoke. I misspoke and that's the end of it. It would have been overkill and totally unnecessary—you have reason enough to owe the girl nothing without even going into what she said about your father."

At Luna Park Virago's blouse got all wet from the Splash Ride, not to mention a dime now already down the drain, and she had to make a stop at a restroom. You see? Have patience and your chance comes on little rat feet, because the second Virago was out of sight I made my break from Camp Chivalry, running as fast as I could to Steeplechase Park, where I plunked down my nickel ad-mission, was forced to take the metal race-horse ride with the danger of its full visibility, and then skulked through the total, safe darkness of the Spook House, where I stum-bled along through twists and turns, passing monster and vampire heads jumping out with these keening shrieks, which were the only sounds I heard for a while, it being a Thursday when school wasn't out yet except for us mackerel snappers who were constantly threatening to take over the government if only some imbeciles in Congress were to sunder the wall between church and state by giving St. Stephen's fifty dollars for books, whereupon we would immediately reinstate burnings at the stake and all the fun we once had with Torquemada, in whose memory we would rename the White House the "Spanish House," all of this, of course, in our "First One Hundred Days." Meantime, turning a corner in the darkness I made a sudden stop and then took a step backward. Someone facing me was blocking my path. I said, "Hey!" I got back silence, and I took another quiet step back. So did he. Or it. Or whatever. I said, "Hey, there! What's up? What's going on?" Still no answer. I was nervous, even starting to be scared. "Come on, who are you?" I hollowly uttered, once again maturely assuming the initiative. Then after another little waiting silence and deciding that I'd had quite enough, I loudly called out, "Brux!" which was a word I'd made up and often used to dispel evil spirits most years of my life, and as none to this date had successfully attacked me, the preponderance of the evidence seemed to say that it worked. Okay, fine, so I admit I took another step backward, which is when this stupid phantom stepped back as well, whereupon I, El Bueno—the staggering genius who, years before, had discovered and announced to his dumbfounded second-grade classmates that "duty" had a meaning unrelated to bowel movements—suddenly realized I'd been talking to a full-length mirror! "Are you just my reflection, you embarrassing, naturally perfected asshole?" I erupted. "My *God,* I feel sorry for you! Really! I feel so sorry I'm going to *puke!*" And then from somewhere up ahead of me—from around another corner, really—I heard somebody sniffling and weeping in the darkness. A child. And then came the frightened cry of a sobbing little girl: "It's too dark in here!"

Well, I fumbled and groped my way through the blackness until finally I got to her. She was huddled on the floor in a corner quietly sobbing into her hands, her little elbows propped on dimpled knees. Dim amber light from a vampire bust on the wall just above her showed her to be maybe about five years old and wearing a light blue calico dress and shiny black patent leather shoes. Obviously a Catholic. "Hey, where are your folks?" I asked her very quietly, afraid of scaring her even more. But at the sound of my voice she abruptly quit crying and looked up at me with a grin. I couldn't quite make out her face but there were pigtails.

"I don't know," she said. "Did my mom send you to get me?"

I said, "No. But I'll bet anything she's right outside. Come on, let's find her."

I reached down and she took my hand and I pulled her to her feet. She was lighter than a sackful of White Castle burgers. She said, "Thank you," and together, hand in hand, we cautiously groped our way out into sunlight and the far cry of gulls and "I'm fucking *soaked!*" from some girl on the Splash Ride at Luna Park. I quickly scanned the area, but no parent, no big brother or sister was waiting. I looked down at her face. Redheaded and freckled, she was smiling up at me. "Your mom should be along pretty soon," I told her. I walked her to a bench and we'd just sat down when a sudden thought unnerved me. What if Vera Virago were to exit the Spook House? *Double dog damn it!* But if someone were to come for the kid, I reasoned, it would have to be here. So we stayed. I kept my eyes on the Spook House exit.

Where was my Barney Google mask when I needed it?

"Don't worry," I heard the kid say.

When I turned my head and looked down at her, she was smiling up at me and softly giggled.

"Don't worry?" I said. "Don't *worry?*"

"No one's coming," she said, looking mirthful. Then she added: "At least not soon."

I now decided to employ that expressionless but subtly accusatory tone that I'd learned from watching all of those Charlie Chan movies. "Ah, so!" I said.

Her little hand flew to her mouth to suppress another giggle. I just stared until her smile went away and she looked solemn. And so what weirdness was this, I was wondering, flummoxed because I wasn't about to ask some four- or five- or six-year-old girl if she read minds for a living or only for her friends, and then . . . "Only for my friends," she piped up. "*Special* friends."

Oh, well, my jaw dropped down to my knees! Was this real?

My amazing seventh-grade intellect, wider than the wingspan of the Inca condor goddess Louise, said I'd have to think of something that would completely eliminate coincidence, and then quicker than Hamlet could dream up his play-within-a-play designed to make his father's killer jump up from his seat in a Perry Mason moment shouting, "Okay, I did it, you fucks! Guard, seize me!"—this followed by a diatribe about the murdered old King Hamlet "stinking up the throne room" with his herring-scented aftershave lotion—I called to mind my seventh-place prize-winning entry in a poetry contest back in third grade and thought to test the kid's telepathic powers by asking her for its title, but then even before I could pose the question *the kid was reciting the poem!*

Said Diana to the Phantom,
'Let's talk on the level.
Who does your laundry?
I know it's not Devil.'

"Kid, who or what are you?" I gasped.

"Oh, for God's sakes, Joey! It's *me!*"

"'It's me?' Who's me?"

"I'm *Jane,* you dumb poop! Your Jane!"

I was stone. I couldn't move. I couldn't talk.

"I really am," she said. "If you'll just look at me closely you'll see."

When the blood had quit pulsing through the vein in my forehead, I stared and, by God! I could almost see it: the freckles, the red hair in pigtails with the smiley-face barrettes at the ends, and then, after she pointed to it, the little circle with the X inside it on her cheek!

There's something wrong with me, I thought.

This was bonkers.

"Oh, come on," she cajoled in her piping voice. "*Gunga Din*, Joey? Blueberry pie and chocolate ice cream? Tokay?"

Nonplussed, I could only gape and numbly nod.

She turned her glance to the exit from Steeplechase Park, then stood up and took my hand. "Come on, let's go," she said. "Vera's coming. She's getting on a big metal horsey right now."

I stood up and said dazedly, "Who paid?"

She said, "Sister Louise. Sister also offered a reward of a dollar for your capture." She tugged at my hand. "Come on, Joey. The boardwalk should be safe for a while. We'll go down to the end where there's almost no people."

That time I'd played the hook at Times Square and right after I'd seen another movie plus live on stage Woody Herman's "Big Band" orchestra with this skinny young crooner Frank Sinatra that these young lolly-dollies in bobby socks were screaming and swooning over with me wondering if all of them were playing the hook too, either that or if they went to some hardcore atheist high school that let them out at noon to get swacked on elderberry juice and cele-brate "Stonehenge Day," right afterward I'd coughed up a shiny new dime to get into an exhibit called "Ripley's Believe It or Not" where I wound up goggle-eyed watching magicians who did stuff that I thought was impossible, which at the time I thought was good, but then afterward thought was bad, for what I wanted was a world with order and complete explanations for everything in it.

But now a pigtailed miracle was holding my hand.

We were walking past a popcorn stand's wafting aromas that were calling to me as seductively as the sirens once sang to Ulysses, *"Here we are, Joey! Come to us! Come! Be the first in your school to commit the sin of gluttony!"* when I stopped and looked down at "Child X." So the kid was telepathic. So what? That didn't make her Jane. Okay? It did not. Further, any kid with money could have bribed our sleazy waiter at that cheapo Italian restaurant into spilling his guts about the blueberry pie and chocolate ice cream. Correct? I mean, isn't that the "scientific method" that's used by every physicist whose last name is Letterman to argue that creation

by a "God" is preposterous, their only answer
to the massive number of "coincidences" making it a virtual impossibility that the universe
wasn't designed for the appearance of man
being, "Idiots! Has it never occurred to you
that there might be an *infinite number* of
universes, in which case there would *have*
to be at least *one* of them with all these coincidences? I mean, *Duuhhhhhhh*!" an expression rendered even more unattractive
when uttered by someone with severe radia-
tion burns on his hands. In the meantime, and
I mention this only in passing, I was almost
dumbstruck into near insensibility by the awe
in which my hero-worshiping young self,
five-time duplicate member of the Doc Savage Club, held the stubbornly dogged and
steadfast faith of all those thousands of scientists who believed that evolution was as
"guided" as a red Ferrari with a drunken and
bitter Ma Joad behind the wheel, and that
after millennia of blindly groping, somehow
nature and chance produced the first chicken,
to which my first reaction was, "*Why,* for
godsakes? Are you *kidding?*" For a time
I stuffed my doubts. Never mind that the

answer from my heroes of science to, "Why would a brain or an eye want to form?" was "To help you survive," with their answer to my follow-up, "Why should I survive?" turning out to be the profoundest and deepest silence since the elderly Rasputin approached Queen Victoria at a palace ball and requested a "private dance." One day I'd mentioned all of this to Baloqui, who, grimacing, then lowering and shaking his head, said broodingly, "Listen, there's a much bigger problem here, Joey," and when I said, "What?" he looked up into the distance with his patented pensively frowning "At least I *think* it was" phony look, and proceeded to ruminate that without an astounding coincidence as yet unclaimed by the Holy Ghost, specifically the appearance of a fully evolved rooster at the very same time, not to mention the very same continent, as the fully evolved first chicken, "Joey, where did the *second* chicken come from?" he said.

Details. Never mind. Science ruled.

So I dredged for more proof that this really was Jane.

"What was the last thing on the East River

walkway that you said to me about my father?" I asked her, and then I instantly threw up an impenetrable wall of white noise around my mind that no telepath could possibly penetrate, a feat that I accomplished by shutting my eyes and mentally reciting over and over the lyrics of the hit song "Three Little Fishies":

Boop boop dittum dattum wattum, choo
Boop boop dittum dattum wattum—

"Joey!"
The kid snapped me out of it sharply.
"I told you that he loved you and to be good to him."
Wham! And then of all the dumb luck, who do I see chatting and coming our way but Baloqui and Winifred Brady! When he saw me Baloqui stopped short for a second, maybe thinking of yelling, "Hey, I've got him! I've captured El Cheapo!" But then the two of them slowly started ambling toward us again. I looked down at Miss Enigma of 1941 and hoarsely whis-

pered, "I thought you said the boardwalk was safe!"

And she hissed back, "Okay, so I *thought* it was safe! I never said I was a fucking oracle!"

My God! I thought. *This really is Jane!*

"Hiya, Joey! How ya doin'?"

Baloqui and Brady were now standing in front of us.

I said, "Fine, Baloqui. Fine. Where's the gang?"

"They're around."

"Yeah, I thought so. Good. That's good."

For a second Baloqui eyed me inscrutably, then he lowered his droopy, dark gaze to Jane. "Who's your friend?"

"You mean you *see* her?"

Baloqui looked up at me, squinting and knitting his brow.

He said, "*What?*"

I said, "I think she's something to see."

Baloqui turned his head to exchange blank looks with Brady, then back to me, his black eyes crammed with suspicion, although of what he as usual had no idea. "You look relieved," he observed. "Why is that?"

"I guess it's just the kind of hairpin I am."

Baloqui shrugged. "Free country."

He returned his gaze to Jane. "So who is she?" he asked.

"My niece."

"You got a niece, El Bueno? Since when?"

"Since she was born," I replied under color of invincible thickheadedness. "She's here visiting from Peru," I then added.

Jane looked down and put a hand to her head and slowly shook it, while, as usual, Winnie Brady continued to say nothing, mutely staring with wide blue eyes, her forte.

"From Peru," Baloqui echoed flatly. He was staring in a way I hadn't seen since that time I was ticked at him over beating me badly at Monopoly and to wound him I'd quoted a made-up travel expert writing in *Holiday Magazine* that Manhattan was "by far a more glamorous, vibrant and exciting city than either Barcelona or Seville," at which Baloqui had lifted his chin and with a look of glacial ice mixed with lukewarm pity said, "Even the Devil can quote scripture out of context." It was the single black eyebrow sickling up that was the killer: it would have turned Lot's wife into a pillar of guava jelly laced with pull-string recordings of her constant "I need my space!" total bullshit, although now she really needed it, you could say.

"Yes, from Lima," I said. And then, after a pause, I quietly added, "Or thereabouts." And at this Jane set up a howl of crying and sobbing.

I looked down and said, "What's wrong, little niece?"

"I have to go baffoom!" she bawled.

His inner vision always turned to an azure sky where puffy cloudlets tinted gold and vermillion by a constantly setting sun framed his pantheon of Apollo, Zeus and Manolete, Baloqui flinched, the corner of his mouth pulling back in a grimace of both fear and distaste at the mention of eliminatory matters, this coupled with a dread of even more to come, such as "ka-ka," or "Da-Vinci Dew," or, worst of all in his mind, "number two," in the presence of Brady in this halcyon, taffy-scented glow of the day. Taking hold of Brady's hand and with a stare in which a clear threat of maiming could be detected, he growled, "That dollar reward's a lot of money, El Bueno. As long as I am silent you are safe. *You owe me!*" With this he turned and they walked away, and with my eyes on Brady's back, in the movie screen of my mind I saw the actor Jack La Rue, always typecast as a gangster, standing beneath a lamppost looking menacing—his only look—while flipping a quarter in the air and catching it over and over, which he did in every movie he was in, his movie dialogue now sounding in my head with a boomy echo-chamber effect:

> "*What about the girl, Baloqui?*
> *She'll talk. Do we kill her?*"
> "*No. I have an arrangement with*
> *a white slaver.*"

When Baloqui and Brady were far enough away, Jane abruptly quit bawling to look up at me deadpan and utter, "I thought they'd *never* leave. Listen, Joey, I'm hungry. Can we eat somewhere now?"

I said, "You *eat?*"

"What does *that* mean?" she said, glow-

ering up at me, and after telling her that I
had no idea, hand in hand we started walking toward a modest little eatery I'd once
seen at the end of the boardwalk where I
thought there'd be almost no chance of another highly dangerous "brief encounter"—
in particular with Vera Virago. I had to take
baby steps so Jane could keep up, and as we
walked I looked down at her pigtails and
curly red mop, still trying to figure out what
was happening. The time jumps. Jane. Were
I older I'd have thought about bizarre dis-
orders of the brain, like in that book *The
Man Who Mistook His Wife for a Hat*, but
back then I was lost. At times I'd just help-
lessly snicker and shake my head, and once
even wondered if I was just dreaming, except
the dream was too long and the Nathan's
aromas too pungent. I mean, I see things and
I've heard things in my dreams but never
smelled them.

This was real.

Whatever *that* was.

10

"Oh, goody!" Jane exclaimed, her eyes beaming in a face as plump and shiny and round as a candy apple held in bright sunlight. Her hand still in mine, she was staring up at the sign for NOT NATHAN'S!!!, the only kosher hot dog server in Coney Island. The sign's exclamation points sent a message:

GOYS, FORGET IT! WE HAVE
NOTHING YOU LIKE!

"What do you want, children? Tell me. I'm here for you."

The paunchy little white-haired, middle-aged guy behind the counter—who I guess was the owner—was wiping his hands on his mustard-stained apron and could easily have been the actor "Cuddles" Sakall, who played the softhearted waiter at Rick's in *Casablanca*. Already his eyes were welling up with forgiveness even before we'd done anything wrong.

He said, "Hot dog? Maybe bratwurst with mustard and onion?"

"You serve any beer or wine?" Jane asked him, her dimpled little face upturned and with her arms akimbo in a classic Shirley Temple mode of challenging sulk. Her voice even had that lispy pout.

The owner's eyes bugged out, and now he looked even more like Sakall saying, *"Honest? Honest as the day is long!"* whereas Jane's defiant comeback stare was more *"You played it for her, you can play it for me!"* "Only root beer, sarsaparilla," he finally sputtered. "But also Joe Louis Punch. I forgot. It's new." He picked up a greenish colored bottle. There was a picture or decal on it of the bare-chested heavyweight champion, the "Brown Bomber," in a fighting stance. The owner held it up to us. "We also have War Cards," he added. These were like baseball cards and came with bubblegum strips, but instead of a photo of Dixie Walker or Cookie Lavagetto on the card there'd be these multicolored comic strip sketches of gory atrocities being committed by Japanese soldiers, things like bayoneting babies in midair and whatever else helped them calm their nerves that day.

"No, no War Cards," I told him. "They'd make the kid sick."

"I understand."

I looked up at a posted menu list with the prices, then leaned over with my mouth very close to Jane's ear. "Have you got any money?" I whispered. She pulled her head away and looked me in the eye with this deadpan, steady expression and said quietly and colorlessly, "Don't you?"

"Uh, well, yeah," I mumbled. "Yeah. Yeah, I guess. I mean, I'm sure. My treat. I insist, in fact. I *insist!*" I straightened up and we ordered some stuff and then took it outside to a bench looking out to the sea. There was a breeze and these jillions of gulls all circling and squawking forlornly but with great agitation and high excitement as if they were in factions that were blaming one another for the loss of some unspoiled world, some paradise where every automobile was a convertible and where hats and awnings did not exist. Meantime, Jane ate a hot dog washed down with sarsaparilla, perhaps if only to prove that she was real and not a ghost like some future scripture scholars, "The Completely Independent-Minded Seminar for the Truth About the Resurrection Scam," as they called themselves, would be saying about Christ, as if the twelve apostles were in fact the Twelve Morons who even in the middle of a sunlit day weren't able to tell a ghost from either Lou Costello or a pepperoni pizza or were just happy to be tortured and killed for what they knew was a lie. The seminar's leader was a celebrated movie director who got famous with *Skyless,* a Norwegian film about a nuclear sub on patrol for three years without ever once surfacing and whose crew members never got irritable or raised their voices to one another. Crammed with subliminal advertisements for Prozac, the movie was a monster hit and the director quickly followed it up with *Sieve*, his controversial "film of supernatural terror" about a condom dispensing machine that's possessed by the spirit of a drill punch. The seminar group used different-colored painted lima beans to vote on the meaning of various enigmatic statements by Christ, such as "Feed the hungry" and "Visit the sick."

God knows what else they did.

"Now, then, Joey, I think we need to talk."

Hands in the pockets of my dashing "genuine Zelan" Windbreaker that I'd whined Pop into buying for me from Davega's on 42nd Street even after he'd explained to me that "Zelan" was a word that Davega's had invented meaning "Nylon for Idiot Children," I turned my soft gaze from the gulls to look down at this pigtailed . . . What? Hallucination? Apparition?

But Baloqui saw her too. Which meant what?

That he was just another part of my delusion?

"Yeah, we *do* need to talk," I agreed.

Boy, *did* we!

"Hold on."

She got up off the bench and with her racing little steps thumping lightly on the wood of the boardwalk, she made a dash to a nearby trash can into which she dumped her napkin, paper plate and the empty sarsaparilla bottle, trotted back to the bench, sat down, clasped her hands in her lap and looked up at me gravely. The bounce of blue light from the ocean tinted her eyes to an aquamarine that seemed much less a color than a memory of seas on some other world.

"Joey, why are you so cheap?" she said.

I almost fell off the bench.

I said, "Huh?"

"You heard me. You're a cheapskate, Joey. The worst! Haven't you learned yet that money can't buy you happiness?"

At this I relaxed a bit, for I was now on familiar ground inasmuch as I was greatly experienced in dealing with "Cliché Experts" and I thought about snappy retorts like, "I presume you are speaking of *Confederate* money," but then decided to be prudent and withhold my friendly fire.

"I've got a few questions of my own," I said.

"Such as what?" she demanded in that piping, sulky voice, her lower lip pouting upward like her muppety doppelgänger/aka Shirley Temple in *Wee Willie Winkie* asking Victor McLaglen why she couldn't go along with him to fight the naughty Thugee assassins who were busy strangling everyone in sight who wasn't wearing a dhoti and a turban.

"Well, for one," I said firmly, "did you or did you not ever float about six feet in the air in front of the refreshment counter at the 'Supe' because they'd just run out of Peter Paul Mounds, not to mention did you ever get into a limo containing the Asp and Mr. Am?"

"Quit trying to change the subject!"

"*I'm* changing the subject?"

Well, at this she launched into her mind-reading thing, which was beginning to resemble Anne Corio at Minsky's Burlesque, flashing quick, sly peeks at her Two Big Reasons at the start of her act to ensure that her audience was fully attentive and understood the point of the proceedings. "And get this straight, by the way," Jane lectured. "The reason clichés are said and written over and over again is because what they're saying is *true!*" Little Jane then went on and on with this theme as she hammered on my "shameful" dealings with Vera Virago, pointing out that at the end of the day all the thrills of the rides and the taste of creamed popcorn would be nothing but a memory and all I'd have is a bunch of regret and self-recrimination, plus a jillion whispered comments made back of shielding hands. "Joey, aren't you even just a little bit sorry? And what would your father think if he knew?"

At that, I decided to listen. *Really* listen.

"Remember that time you were five years old and you found a nickel and a dime in the street in the middle of some thrown-away Alf Landon buttons you picked up because you liked the cheery sunflower on them? You remember what you did then, Joey? You remember? You ran to the five-and-dime," she said, "to the Woolworth's right across the street and you bought a little penknife for your father, a tortoiseshell hair comb for your sister, and got nothing for yourself. You remember?"

My God! She knew *everything!*

I looked out at the ocean.

"Yeah, I remember," I said.

"And how did you feel that night, Joey?"

"I don't know." I shrugged. "I guess happy."

"Was it happy like eating ice cream or even seeing *Gunga Din*?"

No, it wasn't. It had filled me up completely.

I said, "No. Not even close."

Her little eyes were flitting back and forth across my face, and she said, "That's right. When the ice cream and the chocolate are gone, all of that kind of happy goes with them. That's the difference. The other kind of happy stays. So as long as you can smile or say a kind word to someone, you can never run out of giving, which means you can never run out of happy."

A couple of pelicans had flapped their way into the melee of whacko gulls and were dive-bombing vertically into the ocean. Watching them, I nodded my head and said, "True."

"And now you're feeling it all over again a little, right, Joey?"

Again I nodded.

"That was you. The real you. It's still inside you, Joey. See, all you had to do was remember."

I turned my head to look down at her and saw her looking up at me and so pleased. Then she turned to the sea again and the white-flecked foamy surf rolling in. "You like movies a lot, don't you, Joey?"

"Oh, well, sure."

"Did you ever see *The Ghost and Mrs. Muir?*" she asked, a fond faraway dreaminess in her voice. "Maybe not. Maybe it hasn't been made yet. It's about this beautiful young widow who's played by Gene Tierney and she's living in a house overlooking the sea that once belonged to a handsome ship's captain who's played by Rex Harrison and the Captain's ghost begins to haunt her and he falls in love with her, but then this smirky snake, this creepo who's played by George Sanders, he worms his way into her affections. The Captain foresees it will end for her in heartbreak, but he also knows Lucia—that's the widow—well, she has to live her life and he shouldn't interfere, and just before the Captain's ghost disappears for the very last time he looks out through a window at the sea and starts talking emotionally about things they could have done had they met when he was still alive, the great romance and the excitement of the sea and all the faraway places they'd have sailed to together, then at the end of it he breaks your heart when he's still looking out the window and says, 'Oh, Lucia, what we've missed!' "

"And that's the end of the movie?"

"No. It's really the beginning. She grows old and when she dies while she's napping in a chair the Captain's ghost comes back, and taking both of her hands in his, he says, 'And now Lucia you'll never be tired again,' and he lifts her ghost to her feet and she's young and beautiful again and they walk away hand in hand and disappear."

"So what's the point? Are you saying you're a ghost?"

She shook her head.

"Just thinking of what might have been, Joey. That's all."

She fell quiet, a soft and sad kind of quiet,

and I folded my arms across my chest and had joined her in staring out at the sea when a much louder squawking arose among the gulls, infuriated now because one of the pelicans had scooped up a fish and was flying a victory lap around them. "Come on, Jane," I pleaded. "What the heck is going on here! My head's about to split in two!"

"Oh, well, who knows?" she said, sighing, her eyes still on the sea. "Maybe somebody's dreaming us. Maybe it's God: God dreaming this world, this bench, those gulls with their blasé, happy-go-lucky, 'What do we care who we crap on just so long as it's fun' way of thinking. They're just freaking flying sociopaths with beaks." She turned her head and looked up at me intently. "Well, there's one thing that I *do* know," she said, "and it's that the world you're in now isn't the real one. The real one's waiting patiently for you while you make yourself fit to be there and be able to enjoy what it's got to offer. Maybe heaven and hell are the same place, Joey. If it were a restaurant and everything they served had lots of garlic, if you love the taste of garlic it's heaven, but if garlic makes you vomit, it's hell. Life is learning to develop a taste for what heaven's got to offer, and then growing that taste to the max. You know, 'soul formation'? That's really just learning how to be happy, which is learning how to love, *really* love, which is by giving. And then maybe, Joey, one day we'll both be in heaven eating blueberry pie with chocolate ice cream and knowing that we'll never run out of either one, which is just a way of saying we'll have a happiness we know won't ever end. That's the world that you've got to be in training for, Joey, and you get there like Kurt Vonnegut says, which is, '*God damn it, you've got to be kind.*'"

"Who's Kurt Vonnegut?"

She turned to me now with a warm little smile of bemusement. "One day you'll find out for yourself," she said. "In the meantime, just do like he says."

"Okay. Also who's this Rex Harrison?"

"An actor."

"Never heard of him."

"You will."

And it was then I remembered the weird thing that she'd said about that movie, that maybe it hadn't been made yet, and at that a kind of answer to her mystery came to me, the Peerless El Bueno, avid reader of not only *Doc Savage*, *The Avenger* and *The Shadow* while standing for hours by the magazine rack in Boshnack's, but also of *Astounding* and *Amazing* magazines!

"Are you saying you're from the future?" I gasped.

She gave a shrug. "Future. Past. What's the diff?"

"Yes, I see," I said, nodding and looking thoughtful. "Good point."

The little Jane creature eyed me inscrutably, doubtlessly gauging me as brimmingly full of hot peaches, which so often I've been and am and will be. Then she gave a little sigh and leaned back.

"Tell me, Joey," she asked, "are you praying?"

"Yes, I'm praying," I answered her truthfully.

"Every night?"

"Every night."

"'Now I lay me down to sleep'? The 'Our Father'? 'Hail Mary'?"

"The works."

"You're being good to your father?"

"I'm trying."

At this she nodded, big dimples appearing as she smiled and said, "I know. And didn't it feel wonderful, Joey? Didn't it? Just like handing out the gifts that you bought with the fifteen cents that you found."

I blinked. "How did you know about that?"

She shrugged and turned again to the sea. A gentle breeze was drifting in, lightly ruffling her hair as she softly replied, "I just know."

This was now feeling spooky. I felt a fluttering in my chest.

"Jane, what are you? I can't talk about this to anyone else, 'cause if I did they'd want to put me away somewhere. Please, I mean it! It's beginning to make me nervous now. *Very* nervous. Am I dead? Is that it? Am I dead and I just don't know it?"

A warm glint of amusement in her eyes, she turned back to me and fondly sighed, "Oh, Joey." Then she slowly shook her head. "No, Joey, you're not dead," she said, "No way."

But then she had to add, "Not exactly."

I started losing it again.

"Not *exactly,* Jane? Not *exactly?*"

Still bemused, she flipped her Lilliputian hand in dismissal.

"Oh, don't worry. It isn't anything bad. In fact, it's good."

"Being not exactly dead is something *good?*"

"Yes, it's good. Now, Joey, do something for me, would you please?"

"Sure. What is it?"

"I'd love a stick of cotton candy. I want a pink one, not the blue. Would you get it for me, please?"

I just stared. I was "not exactly dead" and she wanted cotton candy. Oh, well, certainly! Right! I mean of *course!* We'd passed a cotton candy cart on our way and I turned and saw the guy and the cart were still there, so I stood up and said, "Sure" just as Jane was slipping a five-dollar bill from somewhere, maybe from behind her ear for all I knew.

I said, "No, Jane. On me. I'm buying."

For a second she just stared. I couldn't tell if she looked pleased or was about to pass out, but then she smiled and said, "Thank you, Joey. Thank you so *much!*"

I'd started walking toward the cotton candy cart when I heard her calling to me and I stopped and looked back. She was facing me and kneeling on the bench, her little hands on the back of it and with her head slightly tilted to the side and the strangest expression clouding her face. Was it wistful? Sad? That old look of adoration when we met?

I couldn't tell.

"You're going to take care of Vera Virago?" she called out.

For a second I was quiet and still. This was heavy.

Then, "Yeah. Yeah, I will," I said at last. "I promise."

She blew me a kiss and as I turned and kept walking I could still feel her eyes on my back. At the cotton candy cart I picked out a pink one, paid, took the stick, turned around and took some steps toward the bench and then stopped. The bench was empty.

Jane wasn't there.

I hurried back to the bench, looking out

at the empty beach and then up and down the boardwalk, and then finally went into Not Nathan's, guessing maybe she'd had to "go baffoom" for real. I didn't see the owner around, so I rapped on the restroom door and when nobody spoke I pulled it open.

No one there.

The owner came out from the back.

"Who are looking for?" he weepily asked me.

I stared blankly, then looked off and said softly, "I don't know."

Outside the shop I stood pensively examining the cotton candy stick I was holding, then looked up at the guy with the cart, assessing the chances of getting my nickel back:

So help me, God, I never licked it even once!

I decided I'd give it to Vera Virago.

11

*Click click click . . . click . . . . . . click. . . .
. . . . . . click . . . . click.*

Like some hideously ugly Romulan mother
ship silently scouring the surface of Earth to
finish off any moaning, wounded survivors
of their initial annihilating attack, Bloor's
shadow fell over my laptop computer.

"So I hear that you used to write movies."

I lifted my fingers from the keyboard.
"Who told you that?" I asked, not daring to
turn because I couldn't risk her interpreting
my stare for a challenge just as you'd have
to with a lion you just happened to run into
at a waterhole out on the Serengeti. This was

something I'd learned just by staring intently at Frank Buck eating.

I heard Bloor answer, "Someone."

"Someone," I echoed dully. "Like my chart?"

"Don't be smart." Then, "What was that?" she said. "You got gas?" I'd quietly groaned because I knew what was coming: an idea for a movie. I'd heard them for most of my adult life: from cabdrivers, barbers, doctors, anyone who's got you trapped for a while, like this dentist in Van Nuys who once tried to get me jazzed about writing a movie about the romance of dentistry, this as he was sharpening a #6 drill and with my mouth propped open as I stared with bulging eyes at the dental horror photos that were plastered all over the wall in front of me: gaping red mouths with rotted and broken yellow teeth, which was what the angry dental god Flosseidon was going to smite you with if you didn't brush twice a day and also come to this dentist's Tupperware parties.

"Tell me, what's your idea?" I asked Bloor miserably.

I wasn't looking for electroshock that morning.

"You've got an idea for a movie script," I added, "right?"

Bloor's eyebrows lifted. "What are you, a mind reader, pal?"

I nodded and blandly answered, "Yes."

This was insolence plain, which she was used to.

"Okay, I'm thinking of a number," she said.

Ah, God! I lowered my forehead into a hand.

"I was kidding," I muttered.

It was a dangerous miscalculation.

"You shouldn't do that," Bloor answered in this unnervingly deadly and quiet tone. I squelched an impulse to shout, *"No, I shouldn't!"* and then maybe *"And Dreyfus was guilty as hell!"* inasmuch as I pictured her with laser beams shooting from her eyes and her hand upraised to plunge a hypodermic needle into my back that was filled with the venom of the Dead Sea anemone which made you say, "Shittier than you by far" whenever somebody asked you how you were feeling. This didn't happen. Instead I said, "Come on! I mean actually I'd *love* to hear your idea."

There was a pause and a silence thicker than tar deeply thinking about freeways and the Problem of Evil. Then I heard the dull click of a stiletto heel as Bloor shifted her weight to her other leg. A good sign. It meant she was relaxing. I had read this in a book about buffaloes.

"Yeah, all I need is a writer to help me with the technical stuff," I heard her say. I turned and faced her. She was standing with her arms akimbo.

"What technical stuff? You mean the screenplay format?"

"No, the words," she said.

I wanted to bury my forehead in my hand.

"And so what movies did you write?" she went on. "Would I know them?"

"Maybe not," I said. "They're really pretty old."

"Well, for instance."

I decided to live dangerously.

"Well, *Tilt*," I said.

"What was that?"

"A sort of theological thriller. These Italian

villagers across from the town of Pisa are jealous as hell because Pisa has the Leaning Tower, which gets all the tourists and the trade, so they kidnap this structural engineering genius and then threaten to throw him and his lucky slide rule into the deepest part of the Tiber tied to "Cement Blocks Marinara con Basilico" unless he figures out a way that they can straighten up the Tower of Pisa."

"Is there a girl?"

"Yeah, Gina. She's the mayor of Pisa's daughter."

Bloor nodded. "Not bad. So what else did you write?"

"*The Fly Six.*"

Bloor's brow furrowed up in surprise. "They made a *Six*?"

"Oh, well, sure! It's the one where by day the Fly is a restaurant inspector for the New York Board of Health."

"That the one with Jeff Goldblum?"

"No. Dolly Parton. I made the Fly a woman for that one."

"Wow!"

"Yeah, that's why I got paid the big bucks."

"No kidding! So now listen," Bloor began as she took a step closer. "About my movie idea. I mean, you really want to hear it?"

"God, *yes!*"

Too much, you think? No. She bought it.

"Well, okay then," she launched. "The plot's about Adolf Hitler. Big name recognition, *kapiche*? Plus I've also got a way to put the story in the twenty-first century, which saves you *mucho dinero* on the budget. No historical sets you'd have to deal with. You couldn't. They've got McDonald's now all over Berlin."

"Yeah, too many."

"Whaddya mean?"

"Just a feeling."

Arms akimbo, head lowered, Bloor inscrutably searched my face for any hint of a dark intent, while in the depths of her eyes rows of slumbering bats hanging upside down began restlessly twitching.

The moment passed.

"Yeah, I get those too," she said, nodding.

"So how does Hitler wind up in this century?" I asked her.

"Well, at first I thought reincarnation."

"Intriguing."

"Doesn't work. Hitler can't be reborn as someone else. He's got to really *be* Hitler."

"What are you getting at? Demonic possession?"

"Kid stuff. The plot's about Hitler's disembodied brain."

"About Hitler's—?"

"Let me finish. What we say is there's these sore-loser Nazi scientists and after Hitler dies they grab his brain and they ice it and they wait for the perfect time to transplant it into the body of an American presidential candidate. In the meantime, while these scientists are twiddling their thumbs they turn into a bizarro kind of ritualistic secret society, wearing monk-type hooded robes and holding lighted candles in the dead of night while they parade in a circle around this freezer containing Hitler's brain and all singing 'I Guess He'd Rather Be in Colorado.' The song's a temp track, by the way. We'll pick one later. In the meantime, this is all taking place in the Arctic, where they've built a base where they can guard the brain. Making sense so far, kiddo?"

"Why the Arctic?"

"Power failures. No danger there the brain would defrost."

Bloor went on to explain how the scientists are foiled by a CIA agent with telepathic powers and who at the end of the film would be revealed to be "an alien being with Jewish interests."

"I see the alien as Tom Hanks, by the way," she finished.

I looked aside, slightly nodding and stroking my chin.

"Yeah, Hanks," I said. "Hanks could be good, Hanks could do it."

"Tom Cruise?"

"Scientology problem. Couch jumper."

"I'd forgotten."

"Humphrey Bogart?"

"He's dead."

"Then John Garfield."

"So is he. Hey, what century are you living in, bright eyes?"

Good question. I didn't know the answer. It didn't matter.

"Now what's hanging me up," Bloor continued, "is where we ought to start the picture. Do we begin with Hitler dying, or do we do that in a flashback so we can start in the Arctic with these weirdos and their ritual thing around the brain? You know, a real grabber like, who are they and why are they worshipping that freezer? What do you think?"

A dangerous moment. First there was that "we." Very chilling. And then what answer could I give her without finally breaking up? I felt like asking for a last cigarette and a blindfold but then flashed back to a meeting one night with Paul Newman in his bungalow at the Beverly Hills Hotel. He was to star in a film I was writing for him and we met to discuss my first draft in which the character's flaws and problems with his marriage and his job are laid out at the beginning (Act One), and then he works through them in the middle (Act Two) while he's shipwrecked on an island, and then at the end (Act Three) he's rescued and comes back home where he deals with all his Act One problems as a deeply changed man. Paul wanted the movie to start on the island, and as being a movie superstar ensconced in a Beverly Hills Hotel bungalow didn't mean that housekeeping wouldn't forget to leave him one or two drinking glasses, we'd been sipping vodka tonics out of a pair of Paul's shoes so that every time I'd woozily protest that we wouldn't know the character had changed unless we knew what he was like *before* then, Paul would lean in his nose about an inch from mine, thus pinning me fast with those icy blues and a Zenlike air of unfathomable wisdom while at the same time struggling to hold his head up as he countered, "Who is to say where Act One should begin?" Which not only shut me up for good but also taught me convincingly that if you want to evade a question or bang the door shut on a topic of discussion, *this* was the line to use, and not that tired old standby, "But then what would Voltaire, or even Montesquieu, think of that?"—this formerly the standard weapon of choice to be mercilessly brandished with impunity since no one will admit they have no clue as to what it might mean. But some exhausted guardian angel ever anxious for my safety must have whispered in my ear that the standard line wouldn't work with

Bloor, and in fact would only baffle and confuse her, thus awakening feelings of inferiority that might even incite her to a murderous rage.

"So come on," Bloor prodded. "What do you think?"

I said, "Who is to say where Act One should begin?"

Nodding her head just a little, Bloor read me inscrutably, then dubiously and quietly commented, "Yeah. Yeah, I see where you're going."

She moved in a step and looked down at my laptop screen.

"That a script you're writing now?"

"No, not a script. A memoir."

"You mean like a book, then."

"Sort of."

"Is it good? Will it sell?"

The danger being minimal, I couldn't resist.

"Well, the truth is I think it could wind up a classic."

"A *classic?*"

"Who knows? I mean, it worked for

James Joyce with *Finnegan's Wake*, and so I'm thinking why shouldn't it work for *me?*"

"So what's the trick?"

"The final sentence of the book is going to end with 'the.' "

She looked surprised. "They let you do that?"

I lowered my head a little, glaring smokily upward like Jack La Rue when the waiter says they're out of pepperoni for his pizza, then said quietly and dangerously, "Who's going to stop me?"

Bloor looked at me blankly, very often an unsettling sign and maybe I'd miscalculated, I feared. But the intercom crackled and saved me.

"Nurse Bloor to the desk! Nurse Bloor!"

"Gotta go. So bottom line: you think my movie idea is commercial?"

Making sure that my brow was furrowed, and in an effort to come off like Sigmund Freud asking Jung, "Are you *positive* these archetypes exist?" I looked off and murmured, "Fascinating. Really. So deep."

What a wretched elitist phony! I knew

very well that executive judgments in the Hollywood studio system were no more well grounded than Bloor's, and perhaps even worse. I once had a screenwriting gig at Columbia's Gower Street lot, where for a time it was the custom for favored writers, producers and directors to take lunch at this huge, long conference table with the studio head presiding, and at one of these lunches he brought up the subject of a rival studio's about-to-be-released motion picture. He had seen its sneak preview the night before at a theater in Sherman Oaks. "Anyone else here see it?" he asked. "No? Well, you're lucky. The picture's a disaster. I'm predicting with total one-thousand-percent accuracy that it won't even earn back its negative cost."

I don't know what got into me then; maybe the dry, crummy meat loaf I'd ordered, or a scene I'd written over and over and couldn't whip, but I spoke up and said, "Sir, what do you base that on? How do you know that?"

The studio head's bushy gray eyebrows lifted. "How do I *know* that, you ask? How do I *know* it? I know it because I'm shifting in my seat the whole picture! I know it from my *ass,* young man! My *ass* tells me!" At which Burton Wohl, then working on adapting his novel *A Cold Wind in August* for the screen, followed up with, "Is it therefore your contention, sir, that yours is the monitor ass of the universe?"

Thirty years later it would be recognized that nobody's ass was telling anybody anything. But that was then and Nurse Bloor was even "thener."

"Nurse Bloor to the desk!" blared the intercom again.

Bloor's eyelids narrowed.

"To be continued," she said.

I heard the crackling of ice forming in my bloodstream.

As she pivoted to leave, Bloor stopped and turned to me.

"I almost forgot," she said. "Twyford, Mackey and Baloqui want to know if you're up for a round of Hearts."

Yes, that's right. Baloqui, too, had made it to his eighties, but sadly he'd succumbed to senility and had checked in the week before. I didn't want to see him like that and stayed away; he'd been too vital a force for such an ending. Fordham Prep had unleashed the latent madman in his soul, most especially in his senior year when in the middle of the night he decided to prowl the corridors of the Hotel Edison where his senior prom had been held, banging hard on guest-room doors and then loudly identifying himself in a voice prematurely deep as "Inspector Cardini of the Vice Squad" before commanding, "Open up! Come on, we know you've got a woman in there!" And if a man in the room answered, "But it's my wife!" he'd come back with, "Sir, your wife is the complainant!" Whoever knew what had been lurking in this Spaniard's heart! After prep school he enlisted in the Air Force—in his view the most dashing of the military services—flew a fighter jet, and after mustering out began flying for United Airlines. This was back in the early days of the "Main Line" when the door to the pilot's compartment was always left open so that the passengers could see that the pilot wasn't dead, this having been found, for some reason, to have a calming, reassuring effect upon the passengers. I'd stayed in touch with Baloqui all my life, and wasn't surprised when he told me how he'd sought, in those open-door days, to ease the boredom of coast-to-coast red-eye flights. He would bide his time, he said, waiting for weather conditions "to be right," and when they were he would cap his teeth with these long plastic vampire fangs that he'd bought at the Hollywood Magic Shop in L.A. and then patiently wait for that rare occasion when, with thunder and lightning in the distance, the eerie blue plasma of Saint Elmo's fire started flashing and dancing around the pilot's compartment, which is when he'd turn his head around and hideously smile, fangs bared, at the passengers.

"Sometimes they'd scream," he'd told me happily.

And now he was here.

"What should I tell them?" Bloor asked.

I said, "Nothing."

She studied my face, and then turned and started walking away. "Yeah, that's probably best," she said. "See you at the Christmas party."

In the meantime, let's get this straight: I am *not* in some kind of "Happydale." Okay?

Sure, it's Bellevue, but I'm not in their psycho ward. That would make things so easy to explain, now, wouldn't it? The time jumps. Jane. The whole deal. But this isn't your standard laughing academy, it's a halfway house between death and Don Rickles, and the facts of my story, if you'd really like to know, are even more complicated than trying to take dental X-rays of a cobra. You *will* understand, though.

Finally.

Wait!

12

For the rest of that day at Coney Island I gave Vera Virago as much of the time of her life as a buck and a half and patience could buy. She wasn't a homely kid, just forbidding. Tall and broad shouldered, very husky, she had a round, ballooning Eskimo face that immediately made you think of blubber, and a long fall of coppery, curly hair framing close-set, beady black eyes that never looked or even stared, they *pierced*, so that the first time you met her you'd figure that some pretty strong Jesuit missionary had just brought her back from the Amazon following a memorable struggle at dockside there for possession of two of her personal effects: "*No*, Vera! *No!* U.S. Customs not allow! Blow gun *bad*, Vera! *No!* Machete *bad!*" There had also been a somewhat disquieting moment on that visit to the Museum of Natural History. While all of the rest of our class had moved on, Virago stood glued with these wide staring eyes looking in at an exhibit about Amazon pygmy headhunters and we had to go back and physically tear her away. She had a heart made of caramel custard, though, but even this could be unnerving to the point of irritation. As I'd mentioned, she was so deeply and neurotically insecure that whatever you did for her, like handing her a Kleenex to wipe catsup off her sneakers, or buying her a nickel paper bag of fries, she'd be totally all scraping and bowing, instantly becoming a Japanese geisha and saying, "Thank you! Oh, thank you so much! You are so kind! You are so very very very very very . . . !" until you wanted to slap her around a few times, or even push half a grapefruit into her face like Jimmy Cagney does to Mae Clarke in *Public Enemy;* but then always, by a monu-

mental effort of will, I would see this Kurt
Vonnegut guy Jane had mentioned sitting
high up in a chair on a golden dais a few
feet above me with a wooden leg and made
up as Sam Jaffe playing Father Perrault
in the movie *Lost Horizon* saying gently,
"Be kind, my son," although sometimes it
wouldn't be Vonnegut, it would be "Cuddles"
Sakall, or even once Humphrey Bogart,
though he didn't say "Be kind" or anything
else, he just kept twitching his facial muscles
sympathetically.

That day I got home from Coney Island
late, but Pop had saved dinner and warmed
it up for me and then sat at the table to
watch me eat. He said nothing, sort of studying me, as usual, and puffing on his pipe and
blowing smoke to the side.

"You have very good time today, Joey?"

"Yeah, I did, Pop."

"Yes," he said, nodding. "I see it in you
face."

Another puff, another blowing out of
smoke.

"I think maybe today you make pray
with your heart."

I'd been lifting my fork but stopped to look at him now with little question marks in my eyes. "Yeah, Pop?"

"Yes, I think so."

Should I tell him about Jane? I wondered.

But the question marks turned into exclamation points: *No! He'll worry and take me to doctors!*

I lowered my head and finished dinner.

Late that night I was sitting on the edge of my bed with an elbow on my knee and the side of my head propped against my fist. I was thinking thoughts. You know: Stuff. What Pop said at dinner. Jane. Me finding the nickel and dime on the sidewalk and excitedly running across the street to Woolworth's, dodging oncoming cars and coming close to getting hit. And then the look on Virago's face on the subway ride coming back from Coney Island when I gritted my entire body and mind and put my arm around her shoulder for a second and gave it a pat and then a friendly squeeze. "Had a real nice time," I half yelled in her ear above the roar of the train, and because of the soft-ness of Virago's voice and the apparently bottomless mercy of God, I didn't hear even one of her seventy-six emotional thank-yous.

But I saw her incredibly happy smile.

And the glow that it gave me and is giving me now.

I got up and knelt down by the side of the bed.

"Now I lay me down to sleep . . ."

13

The next day I had my hands around Paulie Farragher's throat and was squeezing so hard that his face had turned blue, but not blue enough yet to satisfy me. I'd surprised him alone in the office of Joseph Andrews Mortuary, which was right across the street from the St. Stephen's church rear entrance on 33rd and where he worked a few hours a week and therefore wouldn't be wearing that moth-eaten oversized coat so he couldn't do his weirdo "Dutch Defense."

"You miserable potato-eating cretin!" I snarled.

I like to think of it as praying with my heart.

• • •

We'd gone swimming at the 23rd Street pool—me, Jimmy Connelly, Farragher and Tommy Foley. Ignoring the warning voices in my head that were saying, "Go not to the pool today, Joey," I went anyway, meeting up with the others at the pool and thinking maybe my hyperalertness against the chance they might again seek to "safety test" the operational limits of my lungs would serve to keep my thoughts away from Jane and the question of my sanity for a while. I stayed clear of the diving pool so nothing happened. It was on the way home that "The Great and Enduring Farragheronian Evil" occurred when the other guys decided on taking a trolley home, they being exhausted, I suppose, from the intense concentration required while targeting me with thought rays intended to lure me to the diving pool and ultimate immersion in the wetness of things, as I'd caught them all staring at me once so intensely that their eyes were almost popping out of their heads while they seemed to be arguing over something, Foley in particular heatedly insisting, "No, it's got to be the *back* of his head, the *back!*" Anyway, I didn't have the nickel fare and ... Okay, okay, I had it but I didn't want to spend it, so I hitched on the back of the trolley but then had to let go when Farragher decided, it being a nice day, to walk to the trolley's open back window and shoot a glob of spittle straight into my eye, thus preparing me for future studies of the character Iago in Shakespeare's *Othello* and the mystery of utterly unmotivated evil—though for maybe half a second before placing my hands around his throat, I did, in all fairness, weigh and find incredibly wanting his vociferous claim that he'd been aiming at a wasp on my forehead that was crawling toward my eye. I couldn't decide which was worse: his stupid lie, or his wounded whimper that "No good deed ever goes unpunished," a lament not entirely unexpected from the future Cardinal Hayes High School valedictorian who thought the names of the Three Musketeers were Orthos, Bathos and Aramis.

Leave off with that smiling. He had to be destroyed.

I'd marched steadily up Third Avenue with blood in my eyes, plus some phlegm, until I got to the mortuary, where I cupped my hands to my eyes and then pressed them against the darkly tinted glass façade and saw only Joe Andrews, the owner and chief mortician, sitting at his desk against a wall. No Farragher. His father was the superintendent of the building and they lived in the basement apartment, but I knew these were Farragher's working hours. As I began to look away from Andrews, I saw him start kneading and clasping and unclasping his hands, which was what Farragher once told me he always did when surreptitiously breaking wind, meantime coughing or loudly clearing his throat to cover up any sound from his deadly malefactions whenever a client was sitting in the office, or against the possibility that someone might enter the room so quietly he might be unaware of their presence. I shifted my glance to a door that led to the place where morticians do their thing with the deceased and I wondered whether Andrews coughed and fiddled with his hands while he was farting in the presence of the dead. I suppose we'll never know. Meantime, Andrews got up from his chair and headed for the door to the street, so I pretended to be reading his "Coming Attractions" sign in the window while he exited the mortuary and walked across the street to a tiny soda, cigarettes and candy store, perhaps to check on the progress of the Milky Way bar that he'd placed atop the block of ice in the soft drinks bin, so I jumped on my chance like a panther and entered the mortuary, where I found and tackled Farragher as he was exiting a viewing room, and after having fun strangling him for a while I had my fist upraised and ready to pound him into jelly, when all of a sudden I just froze with my fist in midair, thinking:

Wait a minute! What would Kurt Vonnegut do?

• • •

I'm not sure that's why I stopped but I did. I mean, I didn't look down and say, "I love and forgive you, brother Farragher and pray you will amend your evil ways very soon," or any other lunatic stuff like that inasmuch as I still was steamed as hell. I just got up and started walking out of the place and when I'd reached the front office and opened the door to the street, I bumped into Andrews, who was coming back in. "Is there anything I can do for you?" he asked me and I vehemently blurted, "Jesus, *no!*" I walked around for a while, still wondering why I'd pulled my punch, and not getting too much of an answer. I just felt it was wrong, that's all. It was wrong and it made me feel crummy.

I wandered down to the East River walkway. With the weather so nice and this being a Saturday, I couldn't find an unoccupied bench, so I sat on a grassy patch for a while looking out across the river at Brooklyn and thinking of that movie that Jane and I had to suffer through just so we could get to *Gunga Din*, this leading me, of course, to more thoughts about the mystery of Jane. And the mystery of me. I was seeing and hearing things. Right?

Who was that person in the mirror?

Once again, I went to bed that night feeling oddly good; in fact, *extremely* oddly good. At peace, you might say. I slept well. I did get up one time to tiptoe into the living room and slide down a window to shut out the sounds of a Health Bar fight, as they were so loud they might awaken Pop. I turned and glanced fondly at him on the sofa. He was good and he slept well *every* night. Then I thought of something else: when I grew up I wanted to be like Pop. I went back into the bedroom and climbed into bed, and just before falling asleep I could swear I heard someone whispering, "Nice."

14

The time jumps went on for the next five years, and always coincided, it seemed, with critical moments of moral decision, like that time in early June of 1942 right after I'd graduated from St. Stephen's. Pop had checked the cupboard that night after dinner and he gave me some money and a list of groceries to go buy. It could have waited until the next day but we'd run out of orange juice and Pop was anxious I should have it in the morning with my breakfast. He would have gone himself but he didn't want to miss *Inner Sanctum*, his favorite radio show with that creepy creaking door at the beginning and then that shivery voice, "This is Raymond, your host . . ."

A new little grocery store had just opened in the nabe called ABSOLUTE LOWEST PRICES! and as there wasn't any WHATYOUTINK at the end of it, and even though Pop had said, "Go to A and P," I thought I'd save him some money and I went there instead. I arrived as they were locking up for the night, but I put on my most adorably pleading Mickey Rooney checking-into-Boys'-Town wistful face and this older white-haired guy just shook his head and sighed and let me in. While they were pulling together Pop's list, I was waiting at the counter when one of the grocery clerks eyed me and quipped to the white-haired guy, "Well, they'll never get *him* in the draft," at which the white-haired guy turned his head and looked at me sadly, then turned back and said softly, "Yeah, they will." Someone in a hurry placed a bag with Pop's order on the counter right next to another one that had been sitting there next to the store's cash register when I'd first come into the shop and then he quickly moved on while another guy rang up the charge, took my money, and gave me the change. He said, "Here you go, sonny," sliding and pushing a bag into my arms. "Tell your folks we appreciate their business." Going home, as I turned the corner on 31st I tripped over something and I fell and skinned a knee. I still had a grip on the bag of groceries, but as I fell I heard this clinking sound, so when I got up I unfurled the top of the bag to see if anything had broken inside. Then my jaw dropped and my mouth did a Martha Raye:

The bag was full of coins and bills, the grocery's take for the day!

I spent the next twenty seconds staggering around in a daze just like Edward G. Robinson at the end of *Brother Orchid* after taking six slugs to the chest, and I wound up sitting down on the bottom step of a brownstone with my arms tightly wrapped around the bag atop my legs as I tried calculating the height of a pyramid made out of World's Fair hamburgers that the money in the bag would probably buy me! Are we getting the message that I wasn't yet entirely St. Joey of

New York? I knew very well what Kurt Vonnegut would do but I wanted a second opinion, and at the thought the Big Loser flew in from Winnetka and he whisked me to the top of the Chrysler Building, at first handing me some stupid apology that it wasn't the Empire State Building, which was taller, because he'd "lost a Big Friend up there" who'd gotten killed by machine-gun fire from airplanes piloted by "basically decent but incredibly misinformed Christers," and it made him "too sad anymore" to go up there, but the creep didn't even get to make his pitch because I waved him off right away, which of course you think means I was resisting temptation, and that could certainly be true, I suppose, except actually it wasn't, as all it meant was I didn't want a partner, my Basic Wicked Mind having already formulated with astounding feral cunning a devious scheme for keeping the money whereby I would go to the A&P, buy all of the groceries on Pop's list and then carry both the money and the groceries home. What was causing me a smidge of concern about the

plan was the part where I would have to tell
Pop that I'd taken so long because I'd stopped
for a minute to pray at St. Stephen's, where
I was kneeling and alone in the church when
out of nowhere—though it seemed like it
was coming from a holy water font—I heard
this voice saying, "Joey! Walk to the corner,
turn right for exactly twenty paces to a
doorway, open it and there on the ground
of the entrance to the recently shuttered and
partially destroyed Japanese Martial Arts
Academy you will find a paper grocery bag.
Take it! Take it and give it to your father!"
As I sat there on the stoop and mentally
polishing my first rough draft—I was thinking of adding to the end of it: "A plenary
indulgence will be granted for compli-
ance"—when I saw these two coins on the
ground. I thought they must have spilled
from the bag when I fell. I got up and went
over and picked them up and as I stood
looking down at them in my hand I felt my
heart begin to thump very lightly, but also
much quicker, and then came this glow in my
chest and that very same feeling of excited

anticipation as I relived myself running back from Woolworth's with my cheapo little gifts for Pop and Lourdes.

I was looking at a nickel and a dime.

I went back to the grocer's and tapped on the glass of the door and when they saw who it was and I was holding the bag, my God their faces lit up like rockets in a Fourth of July night sky! I saw joy! Joy and relief! The older white-haired man just stared at me, stunned, with his mouth in an O and his hands to his cheeks, and then he rushed to the door, pulled it open and hugged me, saying fervently, "*Thank* you! *Thank* you!" and seeming even happier than Lourdes the day I told her the Armenian ABTINKWHATCHYOUTINK tailor had moved to Arizona. Before leaving, I asked them to recount the money. The white-haired guy said, "No no no no, that's not necessary," but I asked him again and he counted it. I wanted to find out whether fifteen cents was missing. It wasn't. Walking home both my steps and the bag full of Pop's list of groceries felt lighter than a pocketful of four-leaf clovers.

• • •

"Joey, you take very long. I was worry."

"Yeah, Pop, it did take me awhile. But I got there."

Yes. I got there.

15

Over the bunches and the twiddles and twad-
dles of the years that followed, there weren't
any time jumps nor did I ever again see Jane.
But she was out there somewhere: I would
get these picture postcards from places like
East Angola and Sri Lanka with these crazy,
funny oddball messages on them like, "Don't
expect to find Des Moines in Eritrea" and
"Nothing is sharper than a sullen Ubangi's
pout," although sometimes the cards came
with pointed reminders like, "Don't stop
praying!" and "Keep going to confession and
communion!" as well as "Right is so freaking much better than wrong!" They always
seemed to come at a time when I was faced

with some moral decision. There *is* an off chance I'd actually glimpsed Jane once. Just maybe. I've never been sure. I was still living in Los Angeles and writing movie scripts when one day on the set of *Pimp My Bloody Toga*—which according to the Stench Films press release was to be "an intense and shocking reexamination of historical events in ancient Rome"—we were shooting an exterior with the usual cast of thousands grumbling about why they weren't being given "stunt pay" when their health was so at risk from chariot dust and Arabian horse manure fumes, when I got into a row with the director, Reggie Flame, freshly hot off his monster hit, *Illegible*, a film about Caligula's palsied calligrapher. It seems the brand-new "thing" among feature film directors was to shoot an expository scene in a men's room with at least one member of the cast shown standing at a urinal. This was somehow supposed to make the scene feel "real," as if the audience didn't know they were watching a movie and not a live sumo-wrestling match. The vogue had started almost two years before with only one actor wizzing and always with his back to the camera; but when that setup got old, the shot escalated to a tighter angle and more to the side, not the actor's back, so you could see the "set dressing" flowing down the urinal wall, this progression, and the shot itself, to be seen one day in retrospect as the start of the "slippery slope" for movie restroom scenes, for when even the closer side angle shot became a movie cliché, another director upped the ante to *two* actors wizzing at once, while yet another drove the bidding up to *three* and a virtual *pissage à trois* that for a time no one imagined could ever be surpassed for its sheer bravado and *joie de uncouth* until someone thought of showing an *actress* wizzing, and then, driven by some primal and apparently irresistible force of nature, soon after came the shot with the leading actress *wiping,* the expectation being *nothing* could be more real than *that,* and never mind that the shot had not the slightest thing to do with either the character or the plot. And so now while the lighting for the following setup was under way, Flame asked for my help with an improvised scene in which Julius Caesar, while entering the Roman senate on the Ides of March, turns his head to stare with bemused disbelief at twenty-two vestal virgins, extras, squatting and wizzing on the senate floor, which is all the distraction he needed, Flame told me, for Brutus and the other conspirators to smite Caesar with their daggers. He wanted me to give the vestal virgins some dialogue that would serve to keep Caesar staring at them until at least the third knife was driven into his chest. "Maybe bitching about the lack of respect they get," Flame suggested. "New taxes. Fees. Maybe that. Only keep it historically in context." Well, I argued against this to the point of much redness in the face and angry shouting in which the word "Brux" made several key and dramatic appearances until finally Flame backed down, and it was then as I was walking away from the encounter that I heard a female extra in the crowd scene outside the Roman senate shouting, "Way to go, writer! Stand up for your beliefs like you do for your pension plan." I turned and saw the shouter. Standing at the front of the teeming throng, she had her arms raised up and was giving me two thumbs-up, but then she turned and disappeared into the vast and madding crowd. I didn't try searching for her. It would have been stupidly hopeless, though on the other hand I guess you had to think a little bit about the red lettered slogan on the front of this T-shirt that she was wearing. How it made it past Wardrobe and the Second A.D. I have no clue. It said,

LIFE IS HARD BUT THEN YOU DIE

It was the "but" instead of "and" that got me thinking.

The Barney Google mask could have just been a joke.

• • •

As I said, there'd been no more time jumps. None. But as I sit here typing, my memory of everything after high school still has that distancing texture about it, like a story being told secondhand, or maybe even a third. After graduation from St. Stephen's, I somehow got into Regis, an all-scholarship Jesuit high school in Manhattan. Boy, the power of prayers! Maybe not even mine. Beginning in junior year, the Regis "Jebbies" gave us a smattering of scholastic philosophy to buttress our faith, which for me at that time was really more a deep hope—you know, courses in logic and things like a "properly stated" principle of causality, namely "Every finite effect demands an equal and proportionate cause." This so you could answer the village atheists at science-oriented Stuyvesant High and their jibes of, "Well, okay, then, so what caused God?" with your coolly delivered ecumenical reply, "You dumb shits! God isn't finite, not a 'thing'! God is infinite!" This knowledge didn't come easy, as I had to suffer frequent humiliations when the Jesuit who taught the course would repeatedly cross out my name at the top of the essays I handed in and replace it with the name of some infamous heretic. Much later in life, perhaps even more useful than these "arguments from reason" that a benign and staggering intelligence had something to do with the creation of the universe, was the time I heard the wonderfully talented standup comedian Richard Pryor say on stage with both medical accuracy and from a legendary personal experience, "You know, when you're on fire your skin goes to sleep."

Figure it out.

16

Pop died in the summer after my high school graduation, and I heaved with sobs day and night for weeks. I never knew a human body could contain so many tears. I believed him to be happy now and free, so the tears were not for him. They were for me. I just loved him so much. I had no thoughts of college. I would work, I decided, and I went to Los Angeles and lived with Lourdes and her husband, Bobby, for a couple of years. They had a house in the San Fernando Valley where the scent of orange blossoms mixed with that of the loam in flower planters out in front of so many newly built tract houses, and the scent was so sweet and so pure I would deeply inhale it and wonder what I ever could have done to deserve it. Lourdes and Bobby were doing quite well, and worked at Hanna-Barbera. They were movie cartoon artists. I asked Lourdes if it ever made her think about my paint sets, and she grimaced and then she laughed and nodded and said, "Oh, yeah!" She and Bobby had a lot of movie contacts and I wound up with a job as a production assistant at Paramount Pictures. I wanted to act and "do voices" but then little by little I started to write, if only as a way of trying to break into acting. The quickest and easiest path to success, I believed, was the so-called high-concept movie idea. This was basically a dynamite premise for a movie that you could tell to the studio "suits" in a single sentence before they'd give you coffee or water or even an undoctored Vanti Papaya—for example, "Dr. Jekyll and *Mrs*. Hyde," or "Bonnie and Clydene," or "All the men in the world wake up one day to find out that all the women in the world have disappeared." And then the probing queries: "This thing contemporary or a costumer?" or "Is there a part for Asa Maynor?" You were lucky when the questions weren't deeper than that, like, "What happens when the men find this out?" or "How is life supposed to go on? Do the women reappear one day looking better?" Any query at all like these was certain trouble, as was also any ill-advised attempt on your part to adapt the old "total topic shutdown" formula and parry, "Well, now how would Bernard Shaw or Fritz Lang have worked it out?" I made a slew of failed high-concept attempts. One was "Hammacher and Schlemmer are Israeli agents who've been tied to each other for years while hunting Hitler's private secretary, Martin Bormann, and it's the thirtieth anniversary of the start of the hunt and one of them has forgotten."

Nobody liked this.

Another one I pitched was, "God and the Devil meet for truce talks at four in the morning in the Carnegie Deli."

Nobody liked this one either.

Those were the better ones.

It might have helped, I suppose, if I'd also had "high-impact" titles for my stories in the vein of *My Stepmother Is an Alien*, or the film's original title, *Who Knew?* It made me wonder whether *The Brothers Karamazov* would have ever come down to us as a classic if its title had been *The Karamazov Brothers*. Who knows?

I got lucky. Columbia Pictures finally bit: they bought my high concept, paid me peanuts to write the treatment and then, liking it, cashews for writing the script, which was made—and so was I because the film made money, *big* money, which meant I could write a few flops in a row and it really wouldn't matter inasmuch as my name would be forever entwined with that first hugely profitable hit.

I didn't walk anymore. I strutted.

Bad, Joey! *Bad!* Pride *bad!*

Especially the false kind.

I was taught not to strut anymore but to walk, and very slowly at that, by "The King," Elvis Presley. MGM had hired me to write his next film. Wow! Was I not the Himalayan cat's rectum?! This delusional hubris ended when I met another screenwriter at the water cooler, which was far down the hall from my office—an unfortunate distance inasmuch as if I happened to have writer's block on any day, the long walk for water turned into a confidence-killing field because all the offices along that hallway were occupied by writers, and the sound of twenty electric typewriters clattering away at warp speed drove me absolutely bonkers and I would find myself muttering a litany consisting of the two words "Hostile assholes!" as I made the dreaded trips back and forth. But then maybe it was worth it because that's how I met Bill Faye, a middle-aged, heavyset man with a fuzz of gray hair and the milk of human kindness all over his face. He'd written dozens of the trickiest kind of fiction, the short story, for *The Saturday Evening Post* and we got friendly and on breaks we would visit and schmooze. One of those times he took a call from an editor at the *Post* asking if he "had anything in his trunk," to which Bill said, "I'm empty," and the editor said, "Okay, do the boxing one again."

I was green, if not livid, with envy.

"Who are you working for?" I asked him one day.

"Ted Richmond."

"Oh, really? Me too," I remarked. "Nice guy."

An affable and chatty man who said he loved to smoke cigars in his bathtub "or any warm Jacuzzi-type thing," Richmond had turned to producing after years of being Tyrone Power's publicist.

"Yes, he is a nice man," was Faye's answer, the same one he would have given about either Jack Oakie or the Marquis de Sade. I never heard him say anything bad about anyone.

"And so what are you writing?" I asked.

"Oh, it's a boxing thing. *Kid Galahad*. It's for Elvis."

My brow wrinkled up. I said, "For *who?*"

Oh, well, I guess you can imagine how both of us were flummoxed when I said that my script was for Elvis too. It got even worse when we started asking around and it turned out that because of his packed fixed-concert schedule and the need to be sure that by a "date certain" there'd be a screenplay that both MGM and Elvis liked, in addition to me and Bill Faye there were *three other Elvis screenplay writers!*

And this, my dear children, is how El Bueno lost his strut.

And learned to walk very slowly.

● ● ●

Meantime, as almost every detective in a British TV series is constantly saying, "May I have a word?" You think American movies are worse now than ever and getting worse every year? Okay, they stink to high heaven. The old-time studio chiefs *loved* movies. Harry Cohn said he kissed the feet of talent, whereas today most studio executives don't even *like* movies—the only thing that excites them is "the deal." Except for that, though, the suits behind the choices being made these days are the same as back then, except they're forty to fifty years younger. Nurse Bloor isn't out of the mainstream. Fling a Frisbee out a second-floor movie studio window and I promise you that one out of two will hit somebody just like Sam Kaddish, the oldster who once ran Kaddish Studios. He hired me to write a screenplay based on an idea I had pitched and which he liked, but when I'd finished it he called me into his office and told me that he wanted some major changes made in accordance with specific ideas that he had, or that maybe his niece or his granddaughter had, and when he'd finished I just sat there and thought for a while, and then I told him that the changes he'd proposed would be ruinous. "You're telling me you refuse to make the changes?" he huffed, and then hoping to win him over with diplomacy, and pretty much oozing a sympathetic and complete understanding of his views, I said, "I'm sorry, Mr. Kaddish, really very *very* sorry, but I just can't be a party to the mindless destruction of this material." I was fired, and if the grounds were for stupidity, justly. Another writer was hired, a very good one in fact, but unfortunately highly obedient, and he rendered unto Kaddish every change, every scene, every ditsy line of dialogue he wanted and the picture was made and released and lost more money than any other studio film ever made. About nine years later my agent H. N. Swanson, or "Swanny" as he was called, went to see Kaddish, who was looking for a writer to adapt a big bestselling novel for the screen. Swanny had a little black book that he carried around in a jacket vest pocket to remind him of the names of the writers he represented and how much in commissions he was owed on the King James Bible, and he hauled it out now, flipped through some pages, and then looked up and said, "How about Joseph El Bueno?"

Kaddish's eyebrows sickled up in horror and he leaned back aghast, his manicured fingertips gripping the edge of his desktop tightly and his knuckles turning white as, "El *Bueno?*" he thundered. "El *Bueno?* Don't even mention his name in these premises! That phony bullshit artist was connected with the biggest disaster of my professional career!" That's the world I was living in, dear hearts, and while I'm really not sure what that says about me, I not only survived but did well: married a wonderful girl, a set designer; had a house in Encino with a view, and pretty much kept my head down and tried to be good, not exactly a breeze in the movie business with all those gorgeous starlets running around on the loose. But to help me there was prayer of both kinds, Pop's and Jane's, and somehow I managed to skate past the abyss.

Barely.

But a win is still a win.

17

"Okay, Hemingway, here's the problem."

I looked up and saw Bloor. She was standing in front of me, a little paper cup filled with water in one hand, and a cup with a medication capsule in the other. I'd been so lost in what I was writing I didn't hear the dreaded *click-click-click* of the stilettos, or maybe she'd glued rubber to the tips. Does it matter?

I said, "What? What problem?"

"Take your meds first," she said. I did. She relieved me of the empty cups, tossed them into a wastebasket and breathing out, "Two!" slid a chair over facing mine, sat down and bent her head way forward. She looked troubled. "The story's great," she said with passionate earnestness. "I mean our movie. Really. I'm sincere. But now I'm asking myself if it's really believable."

I had to tighten my facial muscles.

"What is it that's so hard to believe?" I asked her.

"Hitler's brain in another body?"

"No problem."

"No problem?"

"No. We just open the picture with a shot of him squatting over a Turkish airport toilet, which is basically nothing but a hole in the ground."

"You getting smart again?"

"No," I said. "Really. It's the hot new movie realism thing. 'Duty shots,' they call them. They're even thinking of doing it on the History Channel. You know people are so cynical these days, they don't know who or what they ought to believe. This takes care of that."

"Really?"

"No question! For example, if you're about to play a scene of the beheading of Mary, Queen of Scots, first you show her on the toilet. Then the audience will know the beheading really happened."

Bloor leaned her head back, appraising me with admiration. "You take my breath away," she said.

"Oh, well." I shyly lowered my gaze.

"I mean, really. Boy, you've sure got all the answers."

"No, not always," I murmured. "Not always."

"Listen, level with me, now."

I looked up and said, "Of course. I always do. What is it?"

"My Hitler movie idea."

I said, "Yes?"

"You think it's really got a chance?"

"You never know."

"Oh, thanks! I was afraid you were just being kind!"

She looked down at my laptop.

"You still working on that book?"

"Yes, I am. It's almost finished."

"That so? Congratulations. Bet you're plenty relieved."

"Pretty much."

"You're sure a wild one," she said, thus revealing that she'd not only read my chart but also the report of the attending psychiatrist.

I looked down, faintly smiling and nodding.

"Yeah," I said. "'Wild as the wind in Oregon.'"

"You know, you're really okay," Bloor told me, leaning back and appraising me with her patented *Little Caesar*, arms akimbo, cocky stance and with her head slightly tilted to the side. "A little attitude at times. Maybe a lot. I pick it up. It's my thing. Like my mother said, 'Rose, you've got the gift: you can always tell bullshit from a pile of dunked Oreos.' But now, you—underneath all the guff you're kind of sweet. You've got a heart. You're okay."

I said, "So are you, Rose."

"I know. So will you help me write my movie?"

I nodded.

"You're a goddamn jewel! I mean, that makes us collaborators, right? What a hoot! So, incidentally, when you finish the book can I read it? I mean, I might have some suggestions. You know, tips. You never know."

"You never know."

"A second opinion."

This coaxed a faint smile to my lips and I nodded.

"Yeah, sure, you can read it, but not until after I die."

Which left out a word at the end.

Again.

"Listen, nobody dies here, Joey. They complain. Mind if I call you that? Joey?"

"No, I wouldn't. In fact it would be nice."

"Then good."

She turned away to leave.

"Until then," she said.

This used to be a threat.

18

Lourdes died. My wife died. I hated Hollywood. It hated me back. I was old, which for the new breed of studio suits meant anyone over the age of thirty. ("How would these geezers know what teenagers want?") I'd never done the party scene or made more than a couple of really true friends out there, at least none who were still alive, so at eighty I packed it in and moved back to New York, where I was shocked to see sunlight falling on sidewalks that once had known only shadow and dust beneath the Second and Third Avenue els. They had now been torn down, so that the streets looked like the Champs Elysées with delicatessens. Other things had changed, although not to the good, and I fell into a deep and quite possibly borderline paranoid interest in newspaper ads for a "Walking Stick for the Elderly New Yorker" that at the press of a conveniently located button turned it into a sword cane fitted with a blade at its end that had been tipped with the venom of the Boston Harbor blowfish, which the ad claimed had killed Albert Einstein. I bought two, one with a dark oak finish and the other in a light bamboo, and thus equipped I filled most of my days with jaunty doddering around the old nabes. The park and the handball courts were still there on 37th and First, but when I went looking for 469 Second Avenue—where Foley and his family used to live in a top-floor walk-up and I used to yell up at him to "Come on down!"—there was no such address, a sprawling supermarket now taking up the whole block. St. Stephen's was different too: it was now called the Church of Our Lady of the Scapular, the even bigger difference being that weekdays and Saturday the doors to the church were now locked, as were the tall black iron gates to the school yard—not only during the summers but also both before and right after school hours. Amazingly, the Madame Monique Arrigo fortune-telling shop was still there, although now with the name "Your Future Told" and, of course, different personnel, and one day for the fun of it, for the insouciant *je ne sais quoi* of it, I walked slowly and carefully up those old brownstone steps and then into the shop to have my palm read by a pretty young blonde wearing heavy eye shadow and golden earrings. She told me that I still had a "very long life" ahead of me in which I could pursue my "true gift," which she said was "accounting." True enough, I suppose. Of course I spent a lot of hours sitting alone on a bench along the East River walkway and remembering things.

Very nice. Very sad as well. But cheap.

• • •

One winter's day I took the BMT to Coney Island. Most things were boarded up, of course, the rides still, the boardwalk empty, and the ocean darkly biding its time. I found the bench where Not Nathan's used to be and sat down and stuffed my hands into the pockets of my coat. It was cold. The sky was cloudy and looking like it wanted to rain. Good fishing weather. The gulls and the pelicans knew it; they were circling very quietly, as if they were planning a sneak attack. My thoughts drifted for an hour or so until I saw a huge four-masted sailing ship silently and gracefully crossing the horizon as if it had slipped through a crack in time. I knew some big historical maritime event was coming up, and thought maybe it was headed to the gathering site, or even to some motion picture filming location. Just then a patch of sky opened up in the clouds so that a narrow shaft of sunlight caught the ship's sails, softly washing them in gold and vermilion, and though my lips barely moved and I didn't at all mean to speak, I could hear myself murmuring almost inaudibly:

"'Oh, Lucia, what we've missed!'"

19

It happened on a freezing day in December, and though I'm not certain it had anything to do with what was to come, I had just read a notice in *Weekly Variety* about the coming relocation from Off Broadway to Broadway of a daring production of *Hamlet* in which the "To be or not to be" soliloquy was staged with Prince Hamlet standing at a urinal with senile old Polonius eavesdropping on him while hiding in a toilet stall. I stared blankly at the print for a while, then decided to get up, put on a thick wool sweater, cap and coat, selected the "away" message on my computer, warning that messages containing the words "elderly" or "spry" would be blocked, left my twentieth-floor condo overlooking the East River and the Brooklyn Bridge and slowly shuffled to Second Avenue and the new supermarket where Foley's apartment used to be. Foley got Parkinson's and died in the charity hospital on Welfare Island. A light, fluttering snow had begun to fall and I cupped my hands to my mouth and yelled up at the ghost of Foley's front window, "Hey, Tommmmmyyyyyy! It's El Bueno! Come on down! Let's play handball and then dunk at Kip's Bay!" People walked past me in both directions. No one looked at me. This was New York. The swirling snowflakes grew thicker, some landing on my eyes and making me blink as I kept squinting up with longing for the childhood I wanted back, and when I lifted my hands for another shout, suddenly my arms felt so weak I had to let them drop. Light-headed. Trouble breathing. And now a numbness in my arm, my left side, pins and needles, and then this pain in my chest. I took a wobbly step forward, then another, and the next thing I was aware of was hearing a distant voice—a paramedic's, I was told— saying quietly, "I think he's dead," and the very next second I was speeding through a narrow, pitch-black tunnel toward this brilliant white light—so much brighter than anything I'd ever seen—at the end of it, just like I'd read in a bunch of books in the "El Bueno Supernatural Book Club," which said also that as soon as I got to the light my whole past life was going to flash before me—every good thing, every bad thing—in just a few seconds and that I was going to be judged, but then someone must have put on the brakes because before that could happen I was waking up in Bellevue's Intensive Care ward looking dumber and even more confused than my wont. The rest I guess you've pretty much heard, except I really had died and been resuscitated, no biggie, then was moved to a ward deemed far more friendly to my at-times unusual statements and behavior. Another ride on the Cyclone.

Now we plunge.

20

On Christmas morning, the day after my rapprochement with Bloor, for the first time ever there was fresh-squeezed orange juice with breakfast instead of the usual powdered mix. I had it in my room, in fact in bed, as I was feeling a bit strange. Just a mood. Outside it was raining and I spent half the morning in bed with the computer bringing my memoirs up to date, which was also the reason that I'd passed on the Christmas Eve party in the Day Room the evening before. Well, mostly the reason. I would sometimes get moody at Christmas. It was childish, I know, even petulant, but I'd grown up without ever getting a Christmas present. Oh, well, maybe once or twice when Lourdes would sneak out to the five-and-dime and buy one of those red mesh Christmas stockings stuffed with bubblegum and candy and things like an eraser or a miniature pencil sharpener and stuff and she'd put it by my pillow while I slept so I'd see it when I woke up on Christmas morning. Poor old wonderful, big-hearted Pop: he just didn't seem to know or even care about traditions like Christmas gifts and buying me a suit every Easter. No biggie, correct? I mean, who really really cared? Not me. In the meantime, I had my book to finish and no time for aimless small talk and punchless punch, so I sat up and typed, but then I stopped as this sudden strong feeling overcame me that I ought to go visit with Baloqui. I tried putting it aside but I couldn't, so I got up out of bed and with the sound of my slippers scuffing against a floor that had been trained to forget whatever it saw or heard in this place, I tentatively slow-stepped into the Day Room where Baloqui was sitting alone at a card table, glassily staring while robotically shuffling a deck of playing cards. For a while I just watched him, feeling sadder than hell, then I went over and sat down with the guy. That ebony head of hair was now shockingly white but the high-cheekboned profile was as chiseled and dramatic as ever, and if only *Wuthering Heights* were to be remade and set in Spain, I was thinking, what a Heathcliff he still would make!

"How's it going, Baloqui? How're you feeling?"

The card movements stopped and he turned his head to look at me, his carriage erect and with his chin at its old haughty angle as his black eyes glittered with suspicion.

"Who are you?" he demanded.

"You don't know me?"

Baloqui's eyebrows bristled inward and he glared.

"If I knew you, why in freak would I ask who you are?" he rumbled threateningly. "What do you want? What's your business? Jehovah's Witness? Drugs? Spit it out!"

Dear God, he's deteriorated badly, I thought.

I shook my head and said, "Nothing. No, no business at all."

"Then why are you bothering me?" he snarled. "Who sent you? Carreras? Yeah, it figures. Well, you go back to him, see, and you tell him I said he can take his whole Plaza del Toros and shove it! I'm finished! I am killing no more bulls for that bastard! I don't care *what* he says they've done!"

I just stared at him sadly, almost wanting to cry, when all of a sudden he burst into laughter. "You big dummy, El Bueno! You still believe practically anything I tell you?" His eyes bright and smiley, he kept on laughing and I started to laugh just as hard. We had a great old time, then, remembering this and going over that for at least an hour, maybe two, and he caught me up on a couple of things, like Miss Comiskey and Eddie Arrigo got married and Miss Doyle had died and he'd gone to her funeral Mass where the hymns she'd requested in a parting note included "Tara's Theme" from *Gone with the Wind,* "Ain't Misbehavin'" and "Take Me Out to the Ball Game."

"Got to finish up something," I told him at last, and I got up and we hugged, with me holding him tightly for a pretty long time.

"So long, Johnny," I said into his shoulder.

"Maybe Hearts tonight?" he asked.

I said, "Sure."

I pulled back and looked into his eyes for a little, then I turned and slowly made my way back to my room, where I got into bed and went back to my book. A little later, about a sentence away from bringing my "Diary of a Madman in Total Denial of His True Rotten Self" up to date, I heard someone clearing their throat from close by. I looked up and saw this woman sitting in a chair at the side of my bed and smiling pleasantly at me. She wore the usual candy-striped uniform and hat of the hospital's nurse's aides.

The paratrooper boots were a bit of a departure.

She smiled, waved a hand and said, "Hi."

My quick glance went to the open door, then back to her.

I hadn't heard her come in.

I said, "Hi, there, young lady. What's up?"

The Bellevue nurse's aides were ordinarily quite young. This one wasn't. Late thirties, I would guess, maybe forties. Red hair. Somewhat pretty. Couldn't make out the color of her eyes. Meantime, I wondered, what was she doing with an old Alf Landon button pinned to one side of her hat and a Wendell Willkie button pinned to the other?

"Are you Mister—?"

She paused to lift a card to her view.

"Mr. Joseph El Boono?" she finished.

"Bueno."

"Sorry, Bueno. Are you he?"

Almost done with the book, I was antsy to get back to it.

"I am," I said curtly. "Now what is it, please? What do you want?"

She lifted upturned hands to the side and smiled.

"Oh, well, everything," she said,

I thought, *What?*

I was squinting at her now. My eyesight had grown a bit blurry. "Look, I'm trying to write," I breathed out with weary patience.

"Oh, my God!" She then gasped. "Oh, my *God!*"

She lifted a hand to her cheek as her mouth fell open and her eyes flared into Betty Boop territory. "You mean you're Joseph El Bueno the famous *movie* writer?" she squealed.

Then she slapped at her forehead. "Duuuh-
hhhh!"

My bleary eyes narrowed with suspicion.
Never kid a kidder. The wildly overdone
bimbo squeal of ecstasy was mockery. But
why?

I glowered. "Come on, what is this? Huh?
What's up?"

"Joey, don't you *ever* know me?"

"What do you mean, 'ever know' you?" I
tried studying her face but the blurriness
had gotten even worse. "I don't know you
at all," I said. "Who are you?"

"It's me."

"'It's me?' Who's 'me'?"

She quickly covered up a giggle with her
hand.

"What's so funny?" I said.

She dropped her hand from her mouth
and said, "You."

I squinted harder. There were dimples in
her cheeks.

"You okay in there, sailor?"

I turned my head and saw Bloor. She was
standing in the doorway with only *one* hand
on her hip, a deliberate sign she had come in

peace. For a moment she eyeballed the turned-off TV, and then shifted a frowning look back to me.

"So what's up?"

"What do you mean?"

"Lots of talking going on in here, Joey."

She was slowly and suspiciously glancing around.

I turned a wild look to the nurse's aide. She was chortling again, this time covering her mouth with both hands.

Bloor didn't see her!

"What's going on in here?" Bloor sniffed. "What's harpooning?" Then her gaze settled back onto me. "You got a little pocket radio or something? Maybe talking to yourself? I'd need to know about that, Joey. Okay?"

"Just reading sentences aloud to check their rhythm."

"You do the characters' voices as well?"

"My forte. I thought I told you I do voices."

"Yeah, that's right," she said, nodding. "When you were a kid."

"Do you see this chair?"

I was pointing at the nurse's aide, who

was on the verge of losing it, with full-blown guffaws now threatening to erupt.

Bloor looked at the chair, then back at me.

"Nice chair. Is this an eye test or the start of a joke?"

"Is there anybody sitting in the chair?"

Bloor stared at me inscrutably for a time, her little eyes glaring up from a lowered head like a baby rhino you'd just cursed with a "Brux."

"This could be scary and discouraging," Bloor said evenly. "If this isn't a joke I'm going to have to have certain professional parties take a look at you again, which might of course mean au revoir to my budding movie career. But if it *is* a joke—and knowing you it probably is—then it isn't in the spirit of our newfound and possibly incredibly fragile relationship. Save the funny jokes for our script."

Nodding solemnly, I said, "I will."

As she left, Nurse Bloor closed the door behind her.

I turned to look at whatever it was in the chair. She was wiping at a laughter tear in the corner of her eye with a knuckle. "Funny woman," she said with half a chortle and half with a touch of fondness.

"Yes, everything's funny to you, it seems," I said grumpily.

"Well, everything is."

I shaded my eyes with a hand, looking down. "Yes, that's right," I said with quiet resignation. "And that's because you're a *ka*, a made-up doppelgänger, a female projection of me. I am talking to no one but myself. I'm really crazy."

"Joey, look at me," I heard the aide say to me tenderly.

I looked up and saw a fond, warm look in her eyes.

I could see now they were green. Jade green.

Of course.

"So you're Jane," I said. "The Jane I made up."

Smiling faintly, she nodded her head and said softly, "Yes, I'm Jane. Your Jane. But you didn't make me up, Joey. *I* did."

"What do you mean?"

"I mean my real name isn't Jane."

At this I frowned a bit, puzzled, and I tilted my head to the side. "Then what is it?" I asked.

"It's Eileen. Joey, I'm your mom."

I just gaped. I couldn't catch my breath. I couldn't speak.

My unconscious must have known that she was telling me the truth because otherwise why had my heart started thumping and why were there tears streaming down my cheeks?

She said, "I've come for you. I've come to take you home."

"W-w-w *what?*"

"Merry Christmas, my Joey."

I held out my arms to her.

"Oh, Mom!"

21

She filled my head with a ton of information in just seconds, but I'll have to set it down here very roughly because I haven't much time, only minutes, and my brain and my heart are exploding suns. The time that I'd died and come back, she explained, at the end of my "life review" it was clear my next stop would be limbo, or maybe the word that she used was "purgatory." Not sure of it, okay? The Other Side. But it wouldn't be in one of the better rooms, so Mom pleaded with God that I should get another chance because she'd died when I was born and wasn't there to give me spiritual formation when I was young, which could have set me up to walk in the right direction. She'd blamed herself for her pneumonia just before I was born! Can you believe it? She said it all happened because of her vanity, insisting against Pop's objections that she had to go out in a freezing storm to buy a couple of barrettes and a "really pretty robe" for her hospital stay. "Oh, please send Joey back to his childhood," she'd pleaded. "I mean, *only if just in his mind,* so I can give him the formation he should have had and that I owe him! A few times when he's little and can be molded, that's all, and *then* you can see what choices he makes or that he *would* have made! Alright? You're God, the God of Abraham and Jacob! You mean you can't be the God of virtual reality?"

"Oh, Mom, you're so beautiful!" I marveled.

She smiled and primped her hair for a second, then got up and came over to the side of my bed and I could swear the room was filled with the scent of mimosa.

"*I guard!*"

"Almost time, Joey. Time to go home. Pop's waiting for you."

"Really, Mom? Pop?"

"Oh, well, of course. He's jumping up and down with wanting to see you. He'd be here now except he had this appointment."

"What appointment? *Inner Sanctum*?"

Still smiling, she nodded, and said, "Something like that."

"What's it like there, Mom? Tell me!"

And now suddenly her smile became that rising of the moon I'd once seen in Jane, her face aglow with a joy she had no words to express but that she knew would never fade, not even long after the sun had grown cold and, beyond, when time no longer existed. She put her head back and her laughter flowed out in warm waves.

"Oh, my Joey, you have no idea! *No idea!*"

After that she looked down at me and placed her hand on top of mine, which I could see but couldn't feel. "Are you ready?" she asked.

"Oh, no, please! A few minutes! Can't I have a few more minutes? I need to finish what I'm writing, Mom! *Please!* Five minutes! Okay, four! Give me four!"

"Go ahead," she said softly. "Do what you can and we'll see."

Well, my fingers fairly flew at the laptop keyboard, completing these final four or five pages, and in parting let me say I'd like to thank my director and my wonderful cast and crew, my niece Emilia, and all the barbers who flew to location that elate a love a life a laugh along the

New York City
December 25, 2010

A Special Tribute

Oh, well, hi! My name is Rose Ellen Bloor and I'm a Registered Nurse at Bellevue Hospital in New York City where it was my privilege to care for the coauthor of this work, Joseph Michael El Bueno, the noted screenwriter and humanitarian who was a two-time winner of the PETA Compassionate Colleague Award, once for "never writing scenes in which a character is shown using a flyswatter," and the other time for "never setting the action of the story in either fall or winter or in Russia at any time of year, thus avoiding the use of wardrobe made of fur." After my collaborator's passing it was both my sad yet supremely satisfying privilege to bring this current work into the light of day, even though it was my choice to leave my part in it uncredited, more or less as a tribute to El Bueno, who in fact performed most of the manual labor on the work—the typing, the writing and so on. My most significant creative contribution, perhaps, consisted of the posthumous editing of the manner in which my character was depicted, which, while originally wholly accurate, I thought to be so cloyingly sweet—in fact virtually heroine worship—that the work might lose its credibility, and so I rewrote those scenes, in fact fictionalizing them by making my character at times seem eccentric, even psychopathically hostile and threatening, thus adding both "color" and the necessary tension that had been curiously absent from the work. I know that Joey—that's what he begged me to call him—would approve. He was always so kind. He once told me he would probably die in some movie theater lobby reading audience preview-card comments at a sneak of one of his films, whereas in fact he passed away while composing the present work, thus explaining the incomplete sentence at the end and which only the inexplicable resistance of the publisher prevented me from completing, my thought being to add the words "Navajo Trail."

Well, at least now you know.

Rose Bloor

TOR

Award-winning authors
Compelling stories

Please join us at the website
below for more information
about this author and other great
Tor selections, and to sign up for
our monthly newsletter!